once
you
know
this

once
you
know
this

Peachtree

emily blejwas

Delacorte Press

Text copyright © 2017 by Emily Blejwas
Jacket art and interior illustrations copyright © 2017 by Jori van der Linde

randomhousekids.com

Educators and librarians, for a variety of teaching tools, visit us at
RHTeachersLibrarians.com

Library of Congress Cataloging-in-Publication Data is available upon request.
ISBN 978-1-5247-0097-3 (hc) — ISBN 978-1-5247-0098-0 (lib. bdg.)
ISBN 978-1-5247-0099-7 (ebook)

The text of this book is set in 13-point New Caledonia.
Interior design by Maria T. Middleton

Printed in the United States of America

10 9 8 7 6 5 4 3 2 1

First Edition

for my family

once you know this

one

Every day Mr. McInnis tells us to imagine our future.

He's been saying it since the first day of school and we're already past Halloween and it's still not working. The boys imagine themselves in the NBA and fight over if you have to be for the Bulls when you live in Chicago. I don't know if any of them believe it or if they're just pretending they won't end up like all their brothers and cousins who don't make it to the NBA or to college or even past the end of the block, where they huddle on the corners like cold pigeons.

The girls don't imagine the NBA. Girls with good voices like Marisol want to be singers, but the rest of us can't think of much. We say we won't have babies young like our moms but deep down we're scared we might.

But Mr. McInnis keeps telling us, like he doesn't know what else to say.

I feel bad for him because he's so nice and it's his first year being a teacher and he came all the way here from Mississippi. But at least he didn't end up in the high school where they lock you in class until the bell rings.

• • •

Mom's waiting for me after school wearing a skirt and lipstick, which makes my stomach drop because she only wears skirts and lipstick when Jack is home. I used to wear skirts until I met Jack and now I only wear pants 'cause I don't want to do anything he likes. I don't call him Dad and he doesn't like that either.

"How was school?" Mom asks.

"Good."

"Good." She tries to turn Tommy's stroller but it gets stuck in a crack because one of its wheels always limps behind the others, like Patches's paw the day we found him. I bend down and pull the wheel over. "Thanks," Mom says. Then she pushes it fast over the rest of the cracks because we have to get to WIC on time. WIC stands for Women, Infants, and Children, but Mom will use our vouchers to buy big, ugly blocks of cheese to make lasagna for Jack. The noodles and sauce are cheap but the cheese is expensive.

• • •

WIC is packed because it always is. All the moms are exhausted and all the kids are bored and all the chairs are hard. The women behind the window pretend they can't see us and act like they work in a regular office. Drinking coffee and laughing on their phones and shopping for sweaters on the computer. Tommy's whining in his stroller because he just learned to crawl and wants to get down. Some of the moms let their babies crawl on the floor but not my mom.

I pull out my notebook to do my homework and it flips to the first page from the first day of school when Mr. McInnis made us write as the first thing *Imagine my future.* That's the only thing on the page. It makes me sad that we let him down. That not one of us can imagine the kind of future he means when he says that. That we all know we'll be on the street corner and at WIC for eternity.

• • •

The grocery store took so long and the bus ride even longer so it's black dark when we get home and too late for lasagna. Jack's nowhere in sight. Tommy and I are starving. My great-grandma Daisy is sitting in the living room with no lights on. "Sorry, Granny!" Mom says. She switches on the lamp with the sticky knob even though she's carrying Tommy and a million grocery bags and lots of them have cans. Granny stares at us like waking up from a dream and seeing some other world than our living room with the cat-clawed couch and the crooked left blind. "Can you sit with her, Brit? While I make dinner?" Her lipstick's rubbed off in the middle but still around the edges like it's trying to hang on.

I sit next to Granny and talk my math problems out loud because voices seem to calm her even though she hardly talks at all. When she first got here she could still make sentences. Most of them were a bunch of mixed-up words that almost made sense, like those puzzles where you have to unscramble the letters to make the word. But now, almost nothing. Granny leans back against the couch cushions and watches my pencil scratch across the paper and the eraser dust fly into the air.

• • •

Mom's nervous walking to school even though it's seven-thirty in the morning and the sun is so bright no one could get away with anything. Plus there are plenty of moms and grandmas and some dads walking their kids to school, too, and two crossing guards, and even a policeman leaning against the hood of his car rubbing his black gloves together. But Mom's always nervous walking. Jack says it's 'cause she's a country mouse and never got used to the city but I don't think the city is supposed to feel like this.

She stops all of a sudden and my stomach floats because Mom never stops. "Is that really you?" she asks. Laila's stumbling onto her stoop, which is covered in leaves because she doesn't believe in raking. She always says she's waiting for the wind to do it and Mom says *You'll spend your whole life waiting, girl.* Laila's wearing silver sunglasses shiny as tinfoil and there's still glitter on her cheeks from last night. She put some on me once and Mom rubbed it right off with a baby wipe. It was embarrassing.

Laila mashes a blue ski cap down on her head but her curls are still everywhere. Bobby pins are hanging from some and all of them shimmer in the sun like new pennies. One time Marisol's cousin called my hair mouse-brown and that's exactly how I feel next to Laila. Like a small, plain mouse. "Miles has a doctor's appointment at eight," she says. "Eight! Why would anyone be open that early?" She digs around in her purse and drops her keys in the leaves.

Mom bends down to Miles, whose scarf is wound around him so many times he looks like a mummy

but he's wearing flip-flops. He stares at Mom with rainy-window eyes. "Don't worry," she tells him. "Next year, I'll walk you to kindergarten."

Laila's trying to light a cigarette while kicking leaves around looking for her keys. "I'll hold you to it," she tells Mom, and the cigarette bounces in her mouth. "Hey, you hear about Chitter-Chatter? You know him, right? Walks that little brown dog with half a tail and picks up trash with a stick? Last night a bunch a—"

"Hey," Mom says. "Tell me later." Laila nods and puffs out smoke through her mouth and nose. She reminds me of a wild orange dragon from a book I had when I was little that I haven't seen since we moved into Jack's house so I guess it's gone now. The dragon blew fire and puffed smoke because he was a dragon and that's all he knew. But deep down he wanted to be peaceful, so every night he snuck out of his cave and crept down to the beach to sit by the ocean. It was so black that all he could see was the white line of foam when each wave crashed on the shore and the shiny stars above.

No one knew his secret except a small crab who watched him from the sand. (The crab was also misunderstood because he pinched people all the time.) One night, the rhythm of the waves lulled the dragon to sleep and some fishermen found him early in the morning and tied a big net around him and started dragging him to the castle. But the crab followed along pinching holes in the net and soon the dragon was free. The story didn't say if the dragon kept going back to the beach at night after that. I hope so.

• • •

Mr. McInnis believes in *cultural arts*. He says because we don't have an art teacher or music teacher or Spanish or French teacher, he has to be all kinds of teachers in one. That's why he makes us sing "This Land Is Your Land" every morning after announcements and the Pledge of Allegiance when all the normal classes are sharpening their pencils. It's ridiculous.

Marisol wishes she was in my class because she also believes in cultural arts but I told her to be

grateful she has Ms. Sanogo, who teaches regular things plus tells real stories like about the time that python got into the well in her village. Still, every morning when we sing *When the sun comes shining, then I was strolling / in the wheat fields waving and the dust clouds rolling,* I close my eyes and picture walking somewhere golden like Kansas, or possibly Nebraska.

Mr. McInnis also believes in *interdisciplinary education,* which means doing a lot of subjects at once. Like learning about Chicago is history and government and economics, which is money and power together. Mr. McInnis writes *Haymarket Riot* on the board and tells us how workers were trying to get rights so they only had to work eight hours a day and the people and police got in a big fight. The boys like the fight with police part. Lots of Mr. McInnis's lessons involve people trying to get rights.

"Any questions?" he asks and Leon raises his hand. "Yes, Leon?"

"Why are we doing all this about Chicago?"

"Because you live here. Don't you want to know about your own city?"

"No."

Mr. McInnis squints, which he does when *approaching something from a different angle.* "Maybe because Chicago is all you know, you think everywhere is the same," he says. "But it's not. Every place is different. If you go somewhere else, it won't feel like Chicago." That sounds good to me but then Mr. McInnis says, "I guess maybe you have to leave a place before you can be proud of it."

I look out the window at the houses on the street behind the school, slumped over and propped up with boards, and try to be proud of Chicago. It's trash day so all the cans are out, but it's the Windy City so half of them are tipped over and papers and wrappers and napkins are blowing down the street like kids running away from their moms at the playground. An old lady is bent over her garbage can, tossing stuff back in. But when she finishes she's not strong enough to lift it back up so she just goes inside.

. . .

I finished my homework way before dinner so I'm lying on my stomach on my bed swinging my bare feet around trying to draw that orange dragon when I hear the music. It's like nothing we ever hear on our block, smooth and kind, and it's loud. Granny's already at the living room window with her palms pressed to the glass. Her breath makes tiny circles on the pane like she's trying to call out.

The sun is white in the sky, still above the telephone poles over the parking lot, and Mom is asleep on her bed with Tommy curled up sweaty next to her chest. "We'll just stay on the stoop," I whisper to Granny.

I put our shoes on and take Granny's hand. I unlock all the locks and we step out. The air has a strange warm line under its cold belly and we can see where the music's coming from now. Some guys in faded mechanic suits are fixing a car down the block. They're speaking some other language and I've never seen them before. They don't know to stay in and stay quiet so they're blasting an old-

fashioned song that sounds like it was dipped in honey so the whole neighborhood can hear it.

Granny walks down the steps without even holding the railing. "Granny!" I grab her hand again but she keeps walking, down the sidewalk toward the beat-up, broken-down car. "Wait!" I whisper. "We can't go down there, Granny. We don't know those guys." She keeps walking. We're a few houses away and one of them looks up. "We can hear the music from the steps, Granny! We have to go back." It's too late. All three men quit working to wait for us.

Granny stops next to the car. "You like the music?" the oldest one asks. His accent is heavy and his teeth are mostly missing and the ones he has are small and pointed and yellow. "Beautiful, no? Bessie Smith. An American classic!"

Granny doesn't even seem to see him. "She doesn't really talk," I say. "Granny, we gotta go back. Mom will be worried."

"Ah, but she can listen," he tells me. "Always she can listen."

The song ends and Granny blinks. The men start

working again. We walk back down the sidewalk and up our three cracked steps and into the house and thankfully Mom and Tommy are still asleep. I bring my dragon sketch to the couch where Granny sits listening to regular night-starting-up sounds: cars gunning and bass buzzing and sirens close and far and random shouts, some happy and some not.

two

Jack crashes through the door in the middle of the night but I pretend none of it's real. Not his elbows bumping down the hallway, not the spitting words or crying, or the worst part: the silence after. It wasn't always like this. He used to try to be nice. Once he even took me to a carnival and spent more than thirty bucks on rides. It got bad when Tommy was born and Granny came to live with us, which happened at about the same time so I don't know which one set him off like a messed-up firecracker. But either way it makes no sense. They're both quiet and sweet and easy. All that noise and neither one even woke up.

• • •

In the morning Jack's gone but he left a red mark on Mom's face. She's drinking her coffee slow. Granny's sitting next to her also drinking her coffee slow. But their eyes are different. Mom has the long-lost eyes and Granny has the nervous horse. My first-grade teacher used to say *actions speak louder than words* but really I think eyes speak louder than words because I've seen a lot of people do things they don't really want to do, but every time you can see the truth in their eyes.

Like when Jack hugs Mom before he leaves and grabs all different parts of her and she hugs him back, she has the icicle eyes. And when Cart Man on the corner growls at the kids who touch his shopping cart, looking and sounding just like a lion with his matted mane, his eyes aren't fierce at all. They're saddest of sad. Like a lion stuck in a cage who wants to be back in the jungle.

• • •

Some of Mr. McInnis's cultural arts ideas are okay but this one is terrible, even worse than "This Land Is Your Land." We're all down at the computer lab learning about our family heritage so we can make a family crest. Mr. McInnis knows the county in Scotland where his ancestors came from and the fabric they used for their kilts. He shows us a picture of the McInnis castle and says the McInnis men were warriors and archers and they still shoot with bows and arrows in the Mississippi woods.

My dad is not a warrior or an archer. His name is Leszek Kowalksi and he met Mom when she was a waitress at an Irish pub across the street from a Polish restaurant where Grandma Jane told me he would sit and calculate and drink shots of vodka from a bottle holding a single blade of bison grass. Mom glared at Grandma when she told me that, about the vodka, but I was happy because then I could think about grass instead of the nothing that was there before. I drew lots of pictures of grass that summer in all different shades of green but I left the bottle out, for Mom's sake.

My dad had a student visa to study some kind of math at the University of Chicago. He tried to explain it to Mom once but she didn't understand it even though she's good with numbers. He had thick blond hair that stood up off his head and a nice smile and a gray coat and was not very tall.

After Mom told him she was pregnant with me, he disappeared. She never saw him again, at the Polish restaurant or anywhere. When she tried to ask the waitresses about him, they pretended not to speak English even though they spoke it to the customers all day. Somehow that part of the story makes Mom the maddest, like the Polish waitresses were the ones who betrayed her. Maybe she thought they would understand because they were also waitresses or because they were women. I don't know.

In the computer lab I have ten minutes for my turn and this is what I learn:

1. Kowalski is the second most common last name in Poland.

2. It is basically the Polish version of Smith.
3. I will never find my dad.
4. Kowalski sausage has made a major impact on the American meatpacking industry.

Back in the classroom I draw a huge sausage on my family crest. It looks weird so I give it a smiley face, which makes it look even weirder. Next to me, DeMarcus White is wearing his white crayon down to the end coloring his whole crest white even though the paper's already white. He looks up and I smile quick and he looks over at my happy hot dog and shakes his head, then goes back to his work. DeMarcus can focus in any situation the way Mr. McInnis says the eye stays calm in the middle of a hurricane. He has seven brothers and sisters so maybe that's why. I've been in class with DeMarcus since second grade and if anyone should be able to imagine their future, it's him.

• • •

After school Mom picks me up with her hair brushed as straight as it can go and held with a plain rubber band. She's wearing jeans, her gray sweater with the hole at the elbow, and no makeup. She looks beautiful and I give her a huge hug. She smiles at me without seeing me. Her eyes are still long-lost. "Want to go to the purple-slide playground?" she asks. "It's so nice out."

"Yeah!" I say and offer to push Tommy's stroller because Mom's holding Scrabble and her arm is linked in Granny's and it's hard to do all that. Mom sometimes brings Scrabble places but we never play. Our school got a *grant* earlier this year and every fifth grader got a brand-new board game. Some of us got Trouble and some got Scrabble but we couldn't choose. Mom played with me once but she didn't notice when Tommy put a tile in his mouth.

He choked on it. It was terrifying. Mom kept thumping him on the back and shaking him upside down and finally she reached in and got it out with her finger. I've tried to think of a word to describe her eyes but I can't. It was like Granny's nervous horse but much, much worse. We haven't played

Scrabble since. I don't know why she carries the game sometimes. Maybe she's trying to get her courage up.

• • •

Mom is as smiley as she gets at the playground. She pushes Tommy in the swing and makes faces at him and he shrieks like babies do. Granny closes her eyes on the bench and lifts her face up to the breeze and doesn't try to wander away once. And when I hang from the monkey bars Mom tickles my bare stomach like I'm a little girl. I laugh not because it tickles but because I'm so happy at that moment.

I used to be happy at lots of moments but then we moved into Jack's house. He tricked me by saying how much I'd love having my own room because I used to share with Mom and he said I could paint it any color I wanted. Mom said, "You know she's nine, right? So she might choose pink." Which was ridiculous because my favorite color has always been yellow. "I'll paint it rainbow if she wants me to," Jack said, but that was a lie because my walls are still the color of an old sock and I don't like having my own room at all. I miss waking up and seeing Mom the very first thing. She used to point at me from her bed and I would point back and our fingers just touched.

We stay at the playground past when we should and I wonder if Mom is thinking about Life Before too. The sky's turning lavender and pretty soon the boys will drive their cars slow through the streets. We walk home with our eyes on the sidewalk and I pretend I'm one of those kids on the news playing in the new park on the North Side, and the potato chip bags are red and yellow leaves I'm kicking up with my brand-name sneakers. I kick at one snagged in a crack but it's really stuck.

At home Mom makes real macaroni and cheese the way Grandma Jane taught her. Grandma taught her lots of things, like how to sew on a button and clean fabric using dish soap and sun and make iced tea that tastes like a place you want to go. And Mom always says it out loud whenever she does any of those things: *My mother taught me that.* Then she gets the cinnamon-and-raisin-toast eyes, which are always warm but half happy and half sad.

. . .

Most of the time Mr. McInnis ignores it when we pass notes in class but sometimes he grabs one on his way down the aisle to remind us that we're supposed to care about school. Today he gets one Sofía drew in marker so when he unfolds it we can all see the outlines through the back.

It's a picture of two men holding hands and one is labeled Mr. McInnis and the other is Boyfriend. Which is stupid because none of us have ever seen Mr. McInnis with a boyfriend. We don't see him anywhere but school. We don't even know where he lives. There are hearts all over the page in all different colors and I wonder how Sofía got so many purples and pinks in her marker box. Did she trade for them?

I look up to see if Mr. McInnis is wondering too but his face is as red as the reddest heart and I look back down. Maybe he does have a boyfriend. Sofía's looking down too. We are all looking down. "Okay,"

Mr. McInnis says. "Page fifty-seven. Subject-verb agreement for indefinite pronouns. Can anyone do the first one?" Someone raises their hand and gets it wrong. No one passes a note for the rest of the day.

. . .

I'm eating Cheerios using the least amount of milk possible so the milk lasts through the weekend. I should eat breakfast at school but for some reason I think it would hurt Mom's feelings. Granny's across from me taking tiny sips of her coffee. I wonder if she's trying to make it last too. She reaches toward me but her eyes are on the plants next door that belong to Odessa Williams.

I only know her name because we got a letter for her once by mistake and I returned it. Jack was mad I went alone. He said her son is one of the worst on our block. Which is weird because Odessa takes such good care of her plants it seems like she would take good care of her son too. But maybe kids don't always turn out like their parents. For Tommy, that's a good thing.

"Do you need something, Granny?" I ask.

Granny tucks my hair behind my ear with a shaky hand, then frowns like my face looked better with the hair hanging over it. It probably did. But then she taps my head and mutters. I tuck my hair tighter behind my ears. She taps my head again in the same spot and like a miracle I know what she means. I run to my room and push around all the junk in my top drawer until I find a barrette with a purple flower on it. One of the petals is missing but it doesn't matter. I stick it exactly where Granny tapped her finger and run back to my chair in the kitchen.

Granny smiles and chirps at the barrette. She sounds like the big blue and gray bird with the Mohawk that always sits in the same tree on the same branch on the way to school. It seems like he's trying to tell me something but when I look at him he looks right back with his eyes black beads and his face pointy and hard. Just like some of the boys at school. Granny's chirps turn a little closer to words and I think I hear "pretty" but I'm not sure.

• • •

Jack's been gone four days and the red mark on Mom's face has faded to the palest yellow. She's mopping the kitchen floor with her jeans rolled up, humming a song. I don't know the song but I hold my breath because the sound is so beautiful that I never want her to stop. Then she stops. "Can you lift your feet up?" she asks.

"What? Oh. Yeah." I lift my feet up and she mops under them. Then I tuck them onto my chair so I won't get her clean floor dirty. It smells like lemons in the kitchen and Tommy's bouncing in the doorway in the seat Laila gave us, laughing when Mom swipes at his socks with the mop. I want to pretend everything's fine but I can't because Jack will come home eventually. Mom sits down at the table to stretch her back. I don't want to break her happiness but I have to.

"Mom," I say and tap one finger as gently as I can on her cheek, the way Granny tapped on my head. "You can't let him do that anymore."

She smiles, keeping her happiness, and I'm relieved. "I know," she says. "I'm making a plan."

Mr. McInnis and Ms. Sanogo each chose one volunteer to change the decorations from Day of the Dead to Thanksgiving in the fifth-grade hall and by the best luck in the world, it's Marisol and me!

"Hey, girl!" Marisol says and hugs me around the neck. I can hear her earrings jingle and smell her strawberry lip gloss and I feel like a baby even though Marisol is seventeen days younger than me. "Just like we planned it, right?" she says and looks around at all the skeletons. We used to celebrate Halloween until some parents somewhere complained and now all the schools do Day of the Dead instead. Marisol says, "Guess it's time to take down all these dead guys."

We start pulling on the skeletons, trying not to break their bones. "This is nasty," I say.

"Yeah," Marisol agrees. "But for real the Day of the Dead isn't nasty at all. It's a time to remember all your loved ones. In Mexico, they get together at the graves and clean them and pray and tell stories. And you leave out the dead people's favorite

foods. We make a little altar at home and Mamá always buys a big bag of M&M's and picks out all the green ones and lines them up in a perfect row for her papi." Marisol jumps up to pull down a high skeleton and his head pops off. "Leave it to this place to put a bunch of bones in a hall and call it Day of the Dead."

I wish we celebrated Day of the Dead so I could make an altar for Grandma Jane. Except my memories are just scraps and I wouldn't even know what kind of candy to line up. And Mom keeps her memories so close they only slip out by accident, like when she's searching in her purse for something else and drops a pen in the parking lot.

• • •

Medicare doesn't want to pay for the medicine to help Granny think clearer. I picture Granny's brainwaves as crazy mountain peaks and the medicine washing over them like a river washes rocks. (Mr. McInnis calls this *erosion*.) But that's probably not how it works. "I don't think you understand," Mom says into her phone. She looks around at all the kids coming out of school and finds me standing right in front of her. "Oh. Hi, sweet pea. Sorry. Just—Yes," she tells the phone and we start walking.

I push Tommy's stroller. He's asleep under a huge winter hat that's over his eyes but Mom's hair is loose and flipping in the wind like trying to get her to have some fun. She keeps swatting it away so she can see where she's going. It's weird to see Mom's hair all wild next to her face, like it's teasing her, and I want to grab it and tie it in a knot and tell it to knock it off. Because how can she concentrate on a plan without Granny's medicine and her hair whipping around like that?

Grandma Jane used to make Mom have fun, but in a nice way. She would turn the car radio up really loud and light her cigarette and dance and laugh and Mom would too. They would roll the windows down because of secondhand smoke but even in winter that car felt warm. I wish I could do that for Mom but we have no car and I can't dance and those cigarettes killed Grandma Jane. "It's just that she can't function without it," Mom says to the phone. "What else can I say? How can I prove it to you?"

• • •

There's so much construction paper I know Mr. McInnis paid for it himself because our school would never have this many choices. If every kid wanted a full orange sheet, we could have it. My whole self feels gentle but I'm not sure why. It could be all the paper or the warm air from the space heater Mr. McInnis snuck in or the silence except for the sound of all our scissors. On the second day of school, Mr. McInnis brought scissors for every kid who didn't show up with some on the first day 'cause their mom couldn't afford school supplies or didn't care or wasn't paying attention to the list.

We're doing Matisse paper cutouts which are always bright colors from nature so Mr. McInnis tried to take us outside. I'm not sure what bright colors from nature we could see in this neighborhood in November but we were happy because we usually only go outside for recess and nobody really plays except on the tire swing but the rope broke last week. The security guard stopped us because it's against school policy to go outside except for recess or a field trip. Mr. McInnis tried to talk him into it but he had trapdoor eyes, which are like pretending to listen when you're actually not. So we all turned around and Kayshaun who was last in line turned into the leader and walked us back.

But Mr. McInnis didn't give us extra math problems or say *Maybe next time* or kick the door. He called it a *temporary setback* and told us about how when Matisse wanted to do these cutouts he was old and sick and lived in Nice, France, where the Mediterranean Sea was the deepest blue and the heat was too bright for him to sit by the pool. So they took him inside and he said *I will make myself my own pool.* But I guess he said it in French. Mr. McInnis showed us a picture of Matisse in an old-fashioned wheelchair with all colors of paper scraps at his feet so we knew he was for real.

Then we all closed our eyes and Mr. McInnis told us to picture the brightest thing in nature we could think of. Lots of kids chose the lake downtown with orange or yellow suns in the sky. But I chose a winter night with a midnight blue sky that I made with blue and black stripes because they don't make midnight blue construction paper. I put a bright white moon in the corner. Then I worried Mr. McInnis would think I was lazy because I was the first one done, but when he looked over my shoulder he said, "Exactly."

three

I usually sleep through Tommy's crying but this time it sounds different. He's catching his breath like he's been crying a long time. I go into his room and pull him out of his crib but then I don't know what to do with him so I stick him back in and he really cries then. Granny's bed is empty and for a second I think she got out even though we have three locks and she's never tried to undo them. I peek into the living room and she's in her usual spot on the couch, staring out the front window at the puffs of clouds hiding the moon.

Mom's on her side in bed, breathing fast and moaning a little like Patches when we found him on the sidewalk last summer. We gave him some milk and his name and he felt better. He ran off to explore the house and the street and I thought he might keep going but he ran back and climbed into my lap and meowed up at me like telling me everything he saw. I loved that. But then he clawed up the couch and Jack put him out one night when we were asleep. I called for him all the next day, through the August heat waving up off the pavement and blocking my throat. But I never found him.

"Mom?" I say.

"Brittany," Mom says in half her voice. "I'm fine. Don't worry."

But she's not fine. Sweat's soaked all the way through her tank top and it's running down the side of her face. I want to smooth her hair back the way she does for me when I have a fever but I'm afraid it will fall out in my hand. She told me that happens sometimes when you don't eat much and not to worry but I'm worried.

Who can help? My heart hammers in my head and Tommy cries harder and I can't concentrate. Granny can't help. No matter what I'll never call Jack. I find Mom's cell in her purse and push Laila's name. "Laila? It's Brittany Kowalski," I tell the message. "Maureen's my mom? She's sick. I need help." I hang up and know Laila won't call me back in time. Sometimes I just know things. I can't explain why but I do.

Mom says never go out at night because bad things happen on the street but I have no choice. I unlock all the locks and run next door in my bare feet and nightie that's too thin and too short. No one's out. The sky looks big and magical. I let myself through the fence and walk up the steep concrete steps to the first-floor apartment. The porch is crowded with all kinds of plants, some round and flowy and some mean. I knock on the green door. The paint's chipped but the color's pretty, like the lake on a sunny day downtown.

Odessa peeks through the front window. Her face is wide and brown with freckles tossed across her cheeks like confetti. She undoes her locks and swings the door wide. She's wearing a Bears sweat-shirt older than me and flannel pants covered in silvery snowflakes that make winter seem like a dream without shovels and ice. "Gracious, child!" she says. "Are you the little girl from next door?" I nod. "What's the matter, baby?" she asks.

"My mom's sick," I tell her. "I don't know what to do."

"Where your daddy at?"

"He's not my daddy and I don't know where he is."

"Okay, wait one minute and here I come." She finds her keys and slips her coat on but doesn't bother with the buttons. She pushes her feet into a pair of men's work boots with no socks and locks the door behind her. When we get inside our house, Granny's still frozen on the couch and Tommy's hys-terical. "Does he have a paci?" Odessa asks. I nod. I don't know why I didn't think of that. "Go find it and give it to him, honey. I'll see about your mama."

I find Tommy's pacifier and he lies down. I stay

with him and rub his back till he falls asleep. It doesn't take long. Then I tiptoe down the hall and peek into Mom's room. Odessa's sitting by her side, smoothing her sweaty hair back. She hasn't seen the nests of Mom's hair in the bathroom trash and I don't tell her about them. She gets Mom to sit up and hands her two pink pills and a glass of water. Mom drinks them, nods, then lays back down. Odessa tucks her in like a kid. "She be all right, honcy," she says when she comes into the hall. "Just a little flu's all."

"I'll stay till morning so you can get some sleep. Then I gotta get back home and mind my twin grandsons. They four years old and they so bad!" She laughs a rumbly laugh and walks me to my room and tucks me in too. I lie awake a long time listening for anything strange and when I fall asleep I dream Granny is across the street in the parking lot and the lace of her nightgown is caught on the fence but then the fence turns into Odessa's ivy plant and Granny pulls free.

I wake up before the sun. Odessa's snoring in the

plaid chair but her eyes pop open when I walk in the room. "Oh!" she says. "I'm glad you woke me." She rubs her hands together and shakes them out. "My nephew Tiny be comin' by to drop somethin' off and I don't wanna miss him."

I sit on the arm of the couch and worry. Jack has people pick things up and drop them off sometimes and Mom hates it. Why'd she tell Tiny to come here? I shouldn't have called Odessa. I glare at her. There's a huge man on our doorstep. "There he be," Odessa says. She opens the door and he hands her a paper bag. "Thank you, doll," she tells him.

"Yes, ma'am."

I follow Odessa to the kitchen. "Did you know Tiny was premature?" she asks. I shake my head. How would I know that? "Oh yes, he was. Puni-est thing you ever saw. Fit in the palm of his dad-dy's hand. We didn't think he would make it. No, ma'am." She smiles at me and sets the paper bag on the kitchen table and I squint at her. "And look at him now! So big and strong!" She laughs that laugh again, then gives me sparrow eyes. "You don't ever know what a person will grow up to be," she says. "You just got to wait and see. People do surprise you."

She pulls two huge bottles of Gatorade out of the bag. They're so cold water spills down the sides and I want to cry, just like the Gatorade. But I don't. "Have your mama drink these, honey," Odessa tells me. "She need to hydrate. One today and one tomorrow."

• • •

This time Mom wakes up when Tommy cries and calls for me. She's still weak but has her whole voice back. She tells me how to make a bottle and I make it and feed Tommy. I change his diaper and put his clothes on and sit with him in the living room while he plays with his toys. Laila comes over and feeds him breakfast and puts him down for his morning nap. "I'm so sorry I couldn't get here last night, Britty-Bug," she tells me. "No one would cover for me, and my boss is a . . . Anyway . . ." I smile. She kisses both my cheeks before she leaves and I breathe in deep because she smells like Grandma

Jane, eyeshadow and smoke. I lock the door behind her.

I'm missing school but I can't leave Mom. I start the book Mr. McInnis assigned even though he gave us till Thanksgiving to finish it. Mr. McInnis got a grant and bought us all our own hardcover copies. It's about a gorilla named Ivan who lives in a shopping mall. Then Tommy wakes up and I turn on cartoons. We usually only watch TV while Mom makes dinner and if my homework's done but today it goes on and on. Tommy's bored because he has a short attention span and shouldn't watch TV. One of the WIC ladies told Mom that (the mean one with too much blush and rocks in the parking lot eyes).

By the afternoon Mom's stronger. She drinks the Gatorade in small sips but makes it through half the bottle before she goes back to bed. I wonder if she's *using time wisely* like Mr. McInnis says and thinking of a plan. But maybe she's too sick for that.

I make a peanut butter and jelly sandwich and think about how Grandma Jane used to buy jars of extra-crunchy peanut butter just for me. She was

a teacher in Alabama and came to Chicago every summer to take care of me while Mom was at work. After she died, Mom got quiet and only bought smooth peanut butter and that's another way Jack tricked me because he got Mom to start talking again. And laughing and going out. Jack took her everywhere, even to the Gold Coast clubs, which Laila says are the best. But then Mom got pregnant with Tommy and everything changed but not in a good way like on the diaper commercials.

Tommy falls asleep on the couch and I finish the book about Ivan who at the end gets out of the shopping mall and makes it to the zoo. I cry when he gets there, not because I'm happy for him. I am. But I cry because I want to get somewhere else too, but I don't know where or how or what to do.

• • •

I wake up smelling pancakes and hearing Jack's voice in the kitchen which gives me the weird feeling of being sick and starving at the same time. Mom's at the kitchen table breaking a pancake into tiny bits and setting them on Tommy's tray and he's eating them faster than she can break them. She gives me a shy smile but I don't smile back because this does not seem like a plan to me. "Hungry?" she asks. I'm leaning in the doorway, thinking about going back to my room.

"Not really," I tell her.

"C'mon, Brit!" Jack's voice sounds like someone turned the volume up too high. "You can't pass up my famous pancakes!"

Here are the things I want to say:

1. Nothing about you is famous.
2. Where were you when Mom needed you?
3. You are making pancakes from a box.

But I don't say anything. I'm really hungry and he knows it so I sit down. Mom puts her arm around my shoulders and squeezes. "Thanks for taking such good care of me," she says.

"Odessa took care of you," I tell her, loud enough for Jack to hear. I see his back muscles clench but he says nothing. "Where's Granny?" I ask.

Mom shrugs. "Still asleep, I guess."

"Well, did anyone check on her?" I stand up so quick my chair bangs backward and falls down. Jack turns from the stove and looks at me like I'm a bear in the zoo and he wonders what I might do next. I give him grizzly eyes because he's *being nice* and won't do anything about it. He turns back to his pancakes and I make a big show of stomping down the hall to Granny and Tommy's room but I should have brought my plate because I'm still starving.

Granny's sitting on a perfectly smooth bed with the pillow in a mound under the covers and I know the sheets are triangle tucked the way Mom does it and says *My mother taught me that.* Granny's in her nightgown, holding her church purse on her lap.

"It's only Saturday, Granny," I tell her. "Church is tomorrow." I know we won't go because we never do but it seems like the easiest thing to say. She lifts her purse a little then sets it back down and stares at it like she's waiting for it to do something. I picture it growing wings and flying out the window like a big black glossy butterfly, thin enough to slip through the bars. I sit down next to her and she shakes the purse a little. "Do you want me to open it?" I ask. She doesn't answer so I slide my hand carefully toward the gold clasp and pop it as gentle as I can but she still startles.

Inside there's a baby hanger from the closet, a toothbrush, my blue-and-white flowered sock that's been missing for a month, three spoons, and a banana. Jack laughs in the kitchen and Granny flinches. I hold her hand and it's cool and smooth and thin like tissue paper. We stare into the purse. I wonder if she's trying to run away. She used to ask us all the time to go home. She would stand at the front door with her coat on but all Mom could say was, "Oh, Granny. This is your home now. You are home."

• • •

The district slashed the transportation budget and I don't know exactly what that means except that we're not going to the aquarium. It's the first time I've ever seen Mr. McInnis frustrated. "I've been preparing them all fall!" he tells Ms. Sanogo, and it's true. We know more about leafy sea dragons than any other fifth graders on the planet.

"You'll learn," she says. "It's always the same." Ms. Sanogo's from Africa but she's a mix of Africa and America now. She wears African shirts puffed at the shoulders like summer clouds, with black pants and dark red lipstick. I'm jealous that Marisol's in her class because I could listen to Ms. Sanogo talk all day. I'd like to curl up in her voice with Patches, wherever he is, and take a nap.

"Why don't you take a breath?" Ms. Sanogo says. "I'm free this hour. I'll finish up for you." Mr. McInnis hesitates. He looks at us, at our science books open to Phases of the Moon, at the white-board, at his shoes, then back at Ms. Sanogo.

"All right," he says. "Thanks."

Ms. Sanogo walks to the middle of the rows of desks, picks up my open book, and sets it back down. "The moon, eh?" she says. "Let me tell you about the moon." The boys sink in their chairs and the girls scribble notes to pass, but I'm listening because of her voice. "In my country, in Cameroon, our moon is not like your moon. It is the same moon but it faces a different direction because we are so close to the equator. Do you know the equator?"

"Yes," I say. I'm the only one who hears the question.

"Good. So that means our Cameroonian moon waxes and wanes from top to bottom instead of from side to side." I actually drop my pencil. "And people tell stories about the rabbit in the moon instead of the man."

• • •

Marisol walked five blocks by herself to get here and she'll be in trouble when she gets home but she doesn't care. Her mom's fighting with her big brother, Tonio, because he ditched school three times last week and spends all his time with a girl named Estella who smokes weed and wears no underwear. I ask Marisol how she knows this about the underwear. She says she just knows and I understand because I just know things too.

Marisol says they're really fighting because Tonio drinks sometimes and her mom is scared he'll end up like Marisol's dad. He got so sad when he drank that he would cry even though he was a grown man and one night he got so sad that he died. Marisol never says exactly what happened. Just that he Ended It All.

We're sitting on my front stoop shoulder to shoulder, shivering in our thin coats. "Did your family used to be happy?" I ask her. "Like, before?"

Marisol pauses. "Yeah," she says. "I think so. Sometimes. Because even though Papi could get so sad he could get so happy too. You know? Like extremes."

"Yeah." I think of Jack, but he's only one extreme. I try not to think about what he'll say when he and Mom get back and find us outside. Granny's watching out the window, but what would she do if something happened? Could she dig down deep and find her scream?

"Papi loved music," Marisol says. "And he was a good dancer. He liked to turn up the Spanish station and dance with Mamá while she tried to cook dinner. But she's the opposite. She feels one way always like a straight line. Sometimes I think it's better to go up and down."

"But the down is so bad."

"Truth."

The moon is huge and almost full over the parking lot. "Ms. Sanogo said that in Cameroon the moon faces a different direction so there's a rabbit in the moon instead of a man," I tell Marisol.

"Really?"

"Yeah."

Marisol tips her head to the left, then to the right. "Ai!" she says and points. "I see it!"

I tip my head like hers. "Me too!"

We laugh and hug each other tight but I'm not sure why. It could be because we found something magic on this tangled-up street or because we're together and not alone or because we like the rabbit so much more than the man or because no matter what happens during the day, the night sky is always good to us.

four

Mr. McInnis forgets to make us sing "This Land Is Your Land," so I know he still feels bad about the aquarium. I stop at his desk before lunch. "I'm sorry about the aquarium," I tell him.

He smiles and shrugs. "Thanks."

"But at least we learned a lot. I think it's really cool that male sea horses have babies," I say and he laughs and my body shivers from head to toe because I'm not used to making anyone laugh, especially someone like Mr. McInnis.

"Well, I haven't given up," he says. "Just need to come up with a Plan B."

"What's a Plan B?"

"It's a plan you make when your first plan doesn't work out."

"Oh." I don't know what to say after that, so I say, "I'm also sorry we can't imagine our future."

Mr. McInnis looks surprised. "You can," he says. "You just have to believe you can."

"Well, I imagine things turning into other things sometimes," I say, thinking of the red and yellow potato chip bag leaves and Granny's butterfly purse flitting out the window. "As practice, I guess."

Mr. McInnis folds his arms and tilts his head and looks at me with his mouth dropped a little, the way we might look at leafy sea dragons if we ever got to the aquarium. "And how does that go?" he asks.

"It works a little."

"Well, keep trying. And you know something, Brittany?"

I shake my head.

49

"I took the liberty of imagining your future for you." I blush but I don't know why. I guess because no one's ever done that for me before, that I know about. "And you know something else?" Mr. McInnis asks. I can't even shake my head. I'm frozen. He leans forward a little. "It's crazy bright."

· · ·

"Lily," Granny says. I'm sitting on the couch next to her doing homework and Tommy's watching SpongeBob and banging his hands on the TV while Mom makes grilled cheese and laughs with Laila on the phone. It's been so long since I heard her laugh and it sounds so good. I wish I was as funny as Laila but nobody is. Granny has universe eyes, staring into the air beyond her. I know she's talking to me because she always calls me Lily. I don't think she knows my name anymore.

"What, Granny?" I ask.

"Don't swing so high." It's been a long time since her voice made a whole sentence.

"Okay, Granny," I say quietly. "I won't." She starts to lean back but catches her breath quick and reaches out. "It's okay, Granny," I whisper. "I'm safe." She looks at me. The universe eyes are gone, replaced with marble in a maze. "It's okay," I tell her again and she mutters something I can't understand, shaking her head. She keeps muttering. I want to call Mom but I don't want her to stop laughing so I just sit there and wait for the muttering to stop. It's a terrible sound, like a car that can't catch on a cold morning.

· · ·

Jack's holding the cell phone bill in front of Mom's face and punching one finger into it because there's some number on there he doesn't recognize. He keeps asking her who she called but she can't remember or see the number anyway because there are a million numbers on the page and they're all so tiny and the page is shaking and Mom's voice is shaking and I am shaking too but I sit on my hands so no one can tell.

"I didn't call anyone," Mom says again.

"Right you didn't. Tell me who."

"I don't know."

"Stop telling me you don't know!" Jack yells and I can see his spit in the air in slow motion like in a movie. Then he shoves Mom into the stove and time catches up. Water splashes from the pot onto Mom's arm and she holds her breath so she won't cry. I know because I'm doing the same thing. Her arm's turning red and puffing up in places. "Great," Jack says. He goes out the front door and slams it.

"Mom," I say in the voice of a small, plain mouse. She doesn't answer. She's at the sink, holding a dish towel under running water. "Mom," I say again. She wraps the towel around her arm, still facing the sink.

"Just leave it, Brittany," she says. "Let it go." I can't see her eyes but I don't need to. Her voice is like nails snapping out of the gun Jack borrowed one time to fix the cracked wood around the window.

"How are you mad at *me*!" I yell, but she still doesn't turn around so I run to my room and slam my door too. I crash down on my bed and cry but not because Jack pushed Mom into the stove and not because she burned her arm. I cry because

Mom lied to me. She is not making a plan. She will never make a plan. Granny has a better plan than Mom and she doesn't even live in real life. I need my own plan like Ivan the gorilla. I need a Plan B.

• • •

I get to school early because I walked myself. Mom didn't want me to but I didn't care. Mr. McInnis is at his desk, sifting through our Frida Kahlo paintings. He smiles when I walk in. "Hey, Brittany. So early today. Everything okay?"

"Yeah. Mr. McInnis? Can I ask you a question?"

He sets down the paintings and turns to face me. He's so clean all the time. His shirts are never wrinkled and his pants always end just above the floor. Is he the perfect size for the pants companies or does he get them hemmed that way? I think of Mom handing over my hemmed sundress last summer and saying *My mother taught me that.* Then I shove her out of my head.

"Of course," Mr. McInnis says. "What's up?"

"How do you make a plan?" I ask. "A good plan. Like a Plan B."

He gives me mother-hen eyes, which is weird because he's a man. "Well, let me think." He sits back and folds his hands in his lap. "I guess any good plan begins with collecting as much information as you can."

"It does?"

"Yes, because the more you know, the better decisions you can make. What kind of plan are you thinking of?"

"Just a . . . plan in general." I tuck my thumbs into the straps of my backpack. "I gotta go get some breakfast," I tell him and he nods.

"Brittany?" he calls when I reach the door and I turn back to see him still facing me with his hands still folded. "Good luck."

• • •

There are dark circles under Mom's eyes when she picks me up at school, carrying Scrabble. I've heard her up at night, watching TV low or cutting coupons in the kitchen. But once I got up for water and she was sitting at the kitchen table with no coupons or scissors or anything. Not even a glass of milk. She had spiderweb eyes and was staring out the window at the black dark. Odessa's ivy plant was waving at her in the breeze and spinning its pot like a ballerina but I don't think she even noticed.

"Do you want to play Scrabble at the park?" I ask, trying to boost her confidence. "We can leave Tommy in the stroller. He won't get the tiles."

"What? Oh." She looks down at the box like she didn't remember she was carrying it. "Not today. We need some stuff. From Dollar Tree."

"Mom?"

"Yeah?"

"It's okay if you want to go to Walmart. I know it's cheaper and I don't mind the ride. Tommy likes to look out the window anyway."

Mom looks down at me and I see tears in her eyes but she blinks and shivers them away like they're from the wind. "Thanks. But Dollar Tree's okay. We don't need much."

At Dollar Tree I have a bad idea. I'm supposed to be getting laundry detergent but I'm standing in front of the notebooks instead. I need one for my

Plan B, to write down all the information I collect. I can't ask Mom because she'll ask questions. I look left and right and left again like crossing the street but no one's around. I choose yellow like *wheat fields waving* and zip it under my coat before I can change my mind.

I've never stolen anything and at the checkout I hop between my feet and give everyone jackrabbit eyes. "Do you have to pee?" Mom asks.

"No." My teeth start chattering and Mom rubs my arms to warm me up.

"Are you cold?"

"No."

"I hope you're not getting sick."

"I'm not."

Finally it's our turn and the checkout girl looks straight at me. "Find everything you need?" she asks. She has a million of the tiniest braids I've ever seen that are twisted around each other and piled on her head like a wedding cake. Her fingernails are painted purple and dotted with diamonds. My cheeks are on fire but I have to see her eyes to

know what she'll do to me. I look up and she winks.

"Brittany!" Mom says.

"What!"

"You're burning up. We need to get you home."

The checkout girl says, "Have a nice day and thank you for shopping at Dollar Tree."

• • •

Mom had to go to the other side of the city so a new doctor could *document* Granny's memory erosion so I go home with Marisol after school. We're in her bedroom eating chips that taste like jalapeños and my mouth's on fire but I'm pretending it's not. Marisol's cousin had to go to court so we're babysitting her daughter Isabella who is four. She's spinning around in circles because Marisol dared her to. Finally she falls down and lies on her back.

"The sky's wiggly," she says.

Marisol laughs. "Just hang on and it'll stop." She's scrolling through a pink iPad Tonio gave her. He didn't say where he got it and she didn't ask.

"The ground's wiggly too. It might spill me off."

"No," Marisol says. "It won't."

She finds the song and hands me one of her earbuds. "Here," she says. "Listen to this one. It's so good it makes me want to cry." All around us posters of singers cover every inch of space like wallpaper until they run into Marisol's little sister's side of the room, which is covered in horses. Marisol's smart enough to be something real like a nurse but I don't say it because at least she has an idea. When I see my future I see the sky on a boring Saturday. White. Blank.

Isabella finally sits up. "Let me listen." I hand her my earbud. Marisol's singing along with her eyes closed. Isabella tips her head for a minute like a bird hearing something far off, then gives the earbud back and lies down to stare at the ceiling.

I think she might be worried about her mom so I say, "What are you thinking about?"

"Nothing."

"Isabella."

"What?"

"Do you want to be a singer when you grow up?

Like Marisol?" Marisol's eyes are still closed but she's added hand motions now.

"No."

I smile down at her. She's rubbing snot from her nose and her pigtails are crooked. I imagine her future the way Mr. McInnis wants us to, as a firefighter, a lawyer, an Olympic swimmer. She's only four. She could still be anything. She could be the one to get out of this place. "What do you want to be?" I ask.

"A dancer," she says. "Like my mom."

five

Getting new notebooks is usually my favorite thing.
When Mom takes me shopping for school supplies
I love it more than Christmas or my Easter basket
or fireworks on the Fourth of July. All those new,
perfect pencils and crayons and more paper than I
could ever use. But my Plan B notebook is different. I've been staring at the first page forever and I
can't think of one thing to write. I will never think
of a Plan B.

Odessa's sweeping her steps so I go out and hold
on to the top of the chain-link fence between us.

Jack'll be mad if he comes home and finds me talking to her but he's always mad. "Hi," I say.

"Well, hey, baby girl. What you up to?"

"Nothing."

Odessa laughs that truck starting up laugh of hers. "Better than mischief, I guess."

I smile because I've never heard anyone say *mischief* in real life. I've only seen it in old books and cartoons. "Odessa?"

"Mmm."

"Have you always lived here?"

"Woo! Seem like it but no. Back when I was a sprout like you I lived on the South Side. Oooh, girl, that was nice." She stands up straight like saluting the memory of it.

"Really? Jack says the South Side's dangerous."

"Everywhere's dangerous now. But back then we had a neighborhood! You know what I'm sayin'?" I nod very seriously, even though I don't. "On Saturday nights we used to dress up. Not the way they do now with everything hanging out but for real! Ooh, there ain't nothin' like a woman in a nice

dress with a line just so." She sets down the broom and moves her hand straight across like the horizons Mr. McInnis is teaching us to draw. He says to put them toward the top or bottom but never in the middle. "And it sway when you walk," Odessa says and waves her hand a little. "And some high heels. Back then we looked just fine. The mens too."

"How'd you get here?"

"Oh, I followed a man, same as anybody. His mama lived on the West Side."

"Odessa? Have you ever made a plan?"

"Sure, baby. Lots of 'em. But you know what they say about plans, though."

"What?"

"You know how to make God laugh? Make a plan!" She laughs again, like thunder, maybe like God himself.

• • •

"Aren't you gonna eat?" I ask Marisol, who drank her chocolate milk in one gulp and is twirling a piece of her hair around one finger.

"No. I'm boycotting Taco Tuesday till they call it something else."

I laugh and it sounds strange coming out of my mouth and I wonder if it's really been so long since I laughed. "But it's tacos."

Marisol shakes her head slow like the middle-school girls do before they jump each other. "No. It's not." I'm glad Marisol's my friend because I'd be scared of her if she wasn't.

The table's packed because the leg broke on the table next to us when a boy from Marisol's class kicked it to prove he really knows tae kwon do so all the girls are crowded in with us and they're all talking about Parent Night, which was kind of like Taco Tuesday because there were no parents. "I heard he paid for all the drinks and food and stuff himself and he even had to pay the janitor extra to stay late," Dahlia says.

"That's so sad," Marisol says.

"Yeah, but like what was he thinking?" Sofía says. "Who wants to go to school at night? I don't even want to go during the day." All the girls laugh and

we're squeezed in so close it feels like a nest but the center of me is cold picturing Mr. McInnis alone in a superclean classroom with our Chagall dream paintings cheerful on the walls and a tray of cookies laid out in perfect rows.

"And no one came?" a girl from Marisol's class asks. "Like, no one?"

We all look around at each other until Kenya says, "We did," and everyone stares at her. "My dad and I." Kenya's so quiet and separate like she's in a different school in her mind but stuck in this one. She almost floats when she walks.

"Was it sad?" someone asks. "Was it weird?" but Kenya shakes her head.

"No. It was nice."

• • •

Jack's pacing around the kitchen like he's waiting for someone but I don't know who because we're all here. I'm sitting at the table doing homework and Granny's next to me, squeezing her left thumb with her right hand. Mom's making spaghetti. She rolls the meatballs slow and careful and for some reason I want to smash them with my fist.

Tommy's playing with a plastic ring from a six-pack of Jack's beer and every time I look at him I think of a turtle trapped and sinking in the lake. Mom and I used to walk along the shore picking up litter so it wouldn't get into the water and choke the turtles. And on the walk back we always looked for sea glass so we ended up with one bag of trash and one bag of sea glass and Mom said, *Just like life.* She always let me keep the sea glass.

"What are you doing?" Jack asks. He's trying to pick a fight.

"Homework."

"No kidding. What kind?"

"Art."

"Don't look like art."

"I'm reading about Gustav Klimt. He never painted a self-portrait."

"Who cares? They should be teaching you welding."

I don't care that he's trying to pick a fight. I don't care about anything. I say, "We're in fifth grade."

"What did you say to me?" The kitchen gets quiet but buzzing at the same time like the headaches I used to get when I had ear infections. "What's your teacher's name again?" he asks.

"Mr. McInnis."

"Well, you tell Mr. McInnis for me that your dad thinks he's a pansy."

"You're not my dad."

He shoves the table at my chest, hard, and it hurts. It hurts Granny too but she just squeezes her thumb harder. Mom picks up Tommy 'cause he starts to cry. She opens her mouth and then closes it again. I might hate her.

• • •

On the first page of my Plan B notebook I make a list of the things I know:

1. Jack is mean.
2. Mom doesn't have a plan.
3. Marisol is my best friend.
4. I hate Jack for putting Patches out.
5. I miss Patches.

I'm not getting anywhere, so I start another list.

1. How can we get away from Jack?
2. We need money.
3. Mom needs a job.
4. Jack won't let Mom work because he says she flirts with all the customers.
5. We need to get away from Jack.

I circle number 5, feeling triumphant. But then I realize number 5 is the same as number 1 and the list just makes a circle and I already knew we needed to get away from Jack and I stole something from Dollar Tree just to figure out something I already knew. I'm suddenly so tired. I hide the Plan B notebook under my mattress and fall asleep with my clothes on.

• • •

Marisol and I are on top of the monkey bars at recess. It's only fifteen minutes long and you have to be quick to get a spot on the monkey bars because all the girls want to sit there. Marisol's smart. She got the bathroom pass one minute before recess and went straight to the playground to save our spot. We're watching our feet dangle above a sea of tiny rocks that line the cracks of the bottom of our shoes. I ask her what a pansy is. I know she'll know because she has an older brother.

"Who said it?"

"Jack."

"Then it means a gay."

"Oh." We're quiet for a minute. "But it can mean something else?" I ask. "If someone else says it?"

"*Sí*. A pansy's a flower too. I know because my tía Gabriella's crazy about flowers and she teaches me them. Pansies she always plants close to wintertime. Like right now. They look real delicate, you know? Like paper-thin. But they can survive even in snow. They are strong, strong." She looks at me. "Like us."

Six

Winter came three days ago with no warning and a bunch of snow but Mom hasn't noticed all my sweaters are too short. When she walks Tommy to the corner store for some milk I pull a kitchen chair to her closet to look for her smallest sweater, the color of a rusty car with Laila's cigarette burn on the shoulder. She doesn't wear it much, she probably won't even notice it on me, and I'm freezing.

The shelves are high and I push my hands back as far as they can go and something clinks, like change for the ice cream truck or Odessa's wind chimes. I feel around and find a small gray plastic bag. The Scrabble tiles. I feel around some more and find the board, still new and glossy and folded in half. Mom's voice is in the living room and I shove the game back between the sweaters and long socks and winter hats.

"Brit? What are you doing in here?" Mom asks. Her ears are red along the edges.

"Nothing. Just looking for a sweater but actually I don't need one." I hop down off the chair, away from Scrabble.

"All of mine will be too big for you, peanut. You need some new ones?"

"Not really, I'm fine."

"I can take you to Goodwill tomorrow."

"Okay. Whatever. My old ones are fine. I have to finish my homework." I slide past her out of the room and down the hall, through the living room, and into my room. I hear Mom sigh and it could be about so many things I don't bother thinking about it. I pull my Plan B notebook out from under the mattress and write on a new page:

WHAT IS IN THE SCRABBLE BOX?

• • •

We're in the middle of what's supposed to be math but Ms. Sanogo can't get any answers out of us, even from the kids who always have answers, like DeMarcus. Because at the beginning of math, the secretary (who listens to gospel music in her headset when the phone's not ringing and sometimes when it is) called Mr. McInnis to the principal's office. Some of the boys oohed at him the way they do to everyone but when Ms. Sanogo came in it felt serious.

Kenya's desk is across from mine and I've never really talked to her but this seems like an emergency. "Kenya," I whisper and she looks up. "You think Mr. McInnis is in trouble?"

She shrugs. "My dad said he went to the school board and asked them to change the field trip policy."

I blink at her because I can't imagine being in a family where they say things like *school board* and *policy* and I don't really know what either one means. "Did they change it?"

Now Kenya blinks at me. "No."

71

"I heard the principal found out he's gay." Dahlia didn't mean to say it that loud but it was one of those quiet moments that come up by accident. Except now it's quiet on purpose.

"All right, all right. Calm down," Ms. Sanogo says. "For all you know Mr. McInnis has just been elected teacher of the year." She picks up a copy of *James and the Giant Peach* that's cracked and facedown on Mr. McInnis's desk. Mr. McInnis is an *amalgam*, which is the Word of the Week. It means a lot of different things put together. Because he tries to teach us probability and how to use semicolons but he still reads to us like we're in kindergarten. He says no one is too old to be read to. Maybe I should read to Granny.

And it works. We calm down. I put my elbow on my desk and my face in my hand and start to fall asleep because Ms. Sanogo's voice is like a lullaby and she's reading lines about a dream that makes me want to dream instead of worry. My eyes are almost closed when the door opens and Mr. McInnis walks in and smiles at us.

• • •

Mom slides the girls' sweaters sizes 10–12 down the rack at Goodwill, checking the tags on some and frowning at all of them while I have an ugly sweater contest with Laila. I found one with leather fringe down the sides and a cowboy riding a bronco and Laila's wearing a Christmas sweater with a tiny red bulb for Rudolph's nose (except it's burned out). She belts out "Rudolph the Red-Nosed Reindeer" (with hand motions) and some of the shoppers look over but most don't.

I'm laughing but Miles is not. He sits on a folding chair with no expression like someone wiped off his feelings with a baby wipe. I look behind me to Mom, holding up a green sweater to the light to see if it's stained, then scowling at it and putting it back. Miles and I could be in one of those movies where the babies are switched at birth. Except he's a boy and six years younger than me and has brown skin like his dad.

Laila finishes the song and bows to Miles and me, her curls tipping over and back and Mom is

suddenly next to me holding a small pile of scratchy sweaters. "Can you try these on? Hopefully at least one of them will work."

I take the pile. "Can I do one more sweater with Laila first?"

Mom sighs. "Brit, we really gotta go. If we miss the 5:05 we won't get home until after dark and Granny's alone and I have to make dinner."

"You mean we have to go because Jack might get there first." Mom squints at me like trying to recognize me and I don't recognize me either. Probably because we've been with Laila all afternoon, which makes me feel tough and careless.

"No. It's because Granny will be home in the dark and Tommy's getting hungry." Her voice comes out steady but her eyes are tree bark. Tommy kicks his feet happily in the cart and I think about pointing this out but Laila jumps in between us wearing a sweater covered in poodles wearing poodle skirts.

"Ha!" she yells. "Beatcha!"

I smile. "You win. I gotta try these on now." I carry the sweaters to the dressing room and try them on

as fast as I can, barely looking. They make a blur of color in the smudged mirror like the impressionists. Except they painted in France and I'm in a dressing room that smells like mice and Jack's breath when he comes home late. I pick two sweaters and hand them to Mom. Laila's still wearing the poodles in poodle skirts. She hugs Mom, then me, then we head to the cash register and the 5:05, where a couple of the men are wearing ties but most aren't. Either way, everyone's eyes are long dark day.

No one gets up for Mom to sit except an old lady with a flowery handkerchief tied under her chin with a huge knot. She smiles at Mom and talks to Tommy in a language I don't know except that I know it's Polish. It's just one of those things. I look at Mom and she knows too and she won't sit down. The lady's showing Mom the seat with her hand that's knuckly and bent from being old but Mom makes her eyes sea mist. The lady gives up and shows the seat to me and I make a big deal about sitting down with a big grin because Mom is being ridiculous. The Polish lady pats my head and for the rest of the ride I pretend she's my grandma because somewhere I have a Polish grandma anyway.

We get home just as the sky gets its pink stripes to switch on the lamp for Granny. Tommy's fussy and I'm tired. In my Plan B notebook, I draw a picture of the Polish lady in her handkerchief with her wide smile and knobby hands and the two sweaters Mom got me blowing out the open bus window. The bus window wasn't really open but Mr. McInnis says there's no rules in art. Then I think of Miles sitting frozen on the folding chair and wonder if Laila ever made it to the boys' sweaters sizes 4–6. I turn the flying sweaters into birds.

• • •

"Brittany." Mr. McInnis is looking right at me and my cheeks turn hot like when Mom used to blow-dry my hair before church. "What did you get for number nine?" he asks.

"Oh!" My voice comes out too loud and a few kids laugh and it takes me forever to find number nine on my page. "Three hundred and five," I say, forcing my voice to be quieter this time.

Mr. McInnis smiles. "Good. Kinda dreamy today."

He goes on to number ten and I go back to thinking about my Polish grandma because ever since I realized I have one I can't stop thinking about her. Does she live in Poland still? Did she move to America to be with my dad? Or did my dad go back to Poland? Does she live in the country or the city? Does Poland have cities? I picture her as the old lady on the bus with the flowery handkerchief because I have no one else to picture but she could look like anyone. She could look like me. Or she could be dead, like Grandma Jane, but somehow I know she's not.

The only way to find her is to look for my dad, who I should hate for leaving Mom and me. I could blame him for us being stuck with Jack and losing Patches and a whole bunch of other things but it's hard because I don't even know him. But I don't have to hate my Polish grandma because she doesn't know I exist. That's another thing I know.

• • •

"I can't put it off till tomorrow," Mom says. "No one has any clean socks." I see the line between her eyebrows crease the way it does when she wants something to be different but can't make it different. I know how that feels and I know it's not her fault Jack didn't give her any money until now so I try not to show how much I just want to stay home and draw pictures of the Polish countryside.

I wait on the cold sidewalk with my hands on Tommy's stroller and watch Mom walk up our steps and unlock all the locks. I can't hear her but I know she's talking to Granny in her smooth voice which is like a mixture of peppermint and the satin hair ribbons Marisol gave me for my birthday. That voice used to make Granny smile but last week Mom used it one morning when she set Granny's breakfast down in front of her and Granny didn't smile or eat any eggs. I thought that was the Worst Sign Yet but I didn't say so because Mom already knew it.

Mom comes back with a big black garbage bag stuffed with almost all our clothes. The box calls them *leaf bags* and I wonder if there are moms somewhere who just use those bags for leaves. Raking them up into huge piles on huge lawns in front of huge houses while the laundry does itself inside. Those bags would probably be lighter with just leaves but maybe not because a lot of anything is heavy. Somehow Mom holds the bag on one shoulder with one hand and does all three locks with the other. "Okay!" she calls from the steps like we're going to the circus and I try to beam a big elephant smile at her.

• • •

Tommy loves the Laundromat. He can stand now (as long as he holds on to something) so he goes back and forth along the bottom row of dryers saying nonsense words and banging his hands on the windows. Every time, he stops at dryer 3 and leans his forehead on the glass and watches for a minute before laughing hysterically. I wonder if my Polish grandma would love Tommy too, even though he's not a Kowalski. If she won't, I'll have to come up with another plan because I'm the only plan Tommy's got.

Mom bought me an orange soda (which the mean WIC lady would not approve of because it has no real juice) and a Snickers bar and herself a cup of coffee at the place next door and we're sitting in pink chairs that are curved like Easter eggs eating our perfect four o'clock snack and watching dryer 3.

"I don't see any difference between that dryer and the other ones," I tell Mom.

"Me neither. But babies are smarter than we give them credit for."

"Was I smart?"

"Of course. You're still smart."

"Mom?"

"Yeah?"

"What was the name of that Irish pub you worked at?"

Mom looks at me but I keep studying the dryer. "Why?"

"Just curious."

"It was called O'Lowry's."

Before I lose my courage, I say as fast as I can, "And-what-was-the-name-of-the-Polish-restaurant-

where-my-dad-sat-and-drank-that-vodka-with-the-bison-grass-in-it?"

"U Stasi."

Now I look at Mom because I can't believe she told me just like that and also because I have no idea what she said. But now she's looking at dryer 3 and so is Tommy, back from his most recent trip to dryer 9.

"How do you spell it?" I ask quietly, like trying to get her not to notice the question.

"*U,* then a space, then *S-T-A-S-I,*" Mom says.

I want to write it down in my Plan B notebook in the biggest letters ever but I don't want Mom to suspect anything so I just keep repeating the letters in my head. The washer buzzes behind us and we both jump. Mom gets up and a red sock I never noticed before flashes at me from dryer 3 like *winning!* and Tommy laughs and laughs and I do too.

Seven

By the best luck ever, Ms. Sanogo's class has com-
puter lab Wednesday afternoons and it's Wednesday afternoon. But we still have forty-three minutes
left of school and Mr. McInnis thinks we can solve
for x. We keep telling him we don't know what x is
but he says that's the point. Half the class is checked
out because half the class is always checked out
and another quarter is checked out because it's too
hard. I'm usually one of the rest who tries No Matter What but today I can't focus on anything.

The bell rings and I move so fast I'm the second

one out the door but Marisol's already there, so she must have been the first one out Ms. Sanogo's door or found some other trick the way she does. She raises her eyebrows and tips her head like a model, then hands me the paper with U STASI in giant letters and the address in her handwriting flowing like a river underneath. I actually lose my breath a little because part of me was sure U Stasi didn't exist, at least not anymore, and it definitely shouldn't be as easy to find as Marisol Googling it at computer lab.

Someone bumps us in the rush and Marisol yells at him in Spanish. "Let's get out of here," she says and I follow her down the steps with everyone yelling and shoving and laughing around us. I keep looking at the paper like Marisol's writing might disappear and she yells over her shoulder, "Why you want to go there anyways?"

I yell, "It's where my mom met my dad."

I can't see Marisol's face because she's still in front of me but I know what it looks like. "Are you looking for him?" she yells back.

I'm not, but it would be weird to say I'm looking for my Polish grandma so I just say, "Yeah."

We get outside and the noise spreads out into the clouds and we can walk next to each other again and hear each other again. "Why do you want to find him?" Marisol asks.

"I don't know. I'm just . . . curious, I guess." I can see Mom waiting for me so we stop and I cram the paper into my coat pocket. Marisol waves to Mom and she waves back and Marisol faces me with absolute eyes, which she does not have often. She even holds the edges of my open coat in her fists like a mom telling a little kid to *please promise to look both ways. Every time.*

"I just want to say that you have a great mom," she says. "And maybe you have a great dad too but sometimes people . . . don't want to be found. You know?" I nod and Marisol takes a deep breath. "And if that happens, it's okay. You'll be okay." All of a sudden I think of Marisol's dad Ending It All and wonder who found him. I hug her as tight as I can.

• • •

On the bus I don't think about anything. I only try not to think about things. Like how I stole five bucks from Jack's wallet on the kitchen table when he was yelling at Mom in the living room and how her palms sounded smacking the wall when he pushed her. And how I'm not sorry I took it but will be sorry if he finds out. And how I've never been on the 82 bus and never been this far from home by myself and could get lost or kidnapped in a heartbeat and Mom would never know what happened to me because she thinks I'm at Marisol's doing a fifth-grade project on the expansion of the universe. Ms. Sanogo tried to talk Mr. McInnis into doing just the big bang but he said we're capable of more than that.

Out the window it looks like my neighborhood repeated over and over. We go into a tunnel that's scratchy at the edges because parts of it are fall-ing off but inside the walls are filled with graffiti so bright and beautiful I actually gasp. I wish the district didn't slash the transportation budget and we could all take a field trip here and Mr. McInnis could point out the window with his palm facing the sky the way he does and say, "See? Art comes in all forms. Art can be anywhere."

On the other side of the tunnel the houses are new and smooth and clean and the graffiti's behind us. The trees are three stories tall and some of them bend their branches over the street like giving extra shade. There are lots of colors besides brown and none of the windows are broken, or even cracked. The whole street looks like it got a bath this morning with some kind of special soap. Even the name of the street's different now.

But then we get to my stop and the city switches back to real life like it knew I was coming. The driver's looking in his mirror to make sure I'm paying attention and when I get to the front he says, "Have a good visit, my friend." I told him I was going to see my grandma so that's another person I lied to and I'm sorry because he has a kind face that seems ancient, like out of an old storybook, and his eyes

are dark and sparkly. Also I showed up on his bus with five bucks and no clue and he got me all the way here plus a ticket home.

"You can catch the 56 right there," he says, pointing to the corner. "It will be five minutes at most for the ride so watch closely for your stop." I want to hug him but I know it would be weird so I just say, "Thanks." A crazy thing about life is that most people will never know what they mean to you.

• • •

I didn't think I'd really get here. I thought I'd chicken out or miss my stop or the bus would break down or someone would catch me or U Stasi would be boarded up with a faded sign on the side like a drugstore no one wants anymore. But inside everything's alive. It's lunchtime and people are laughing and drinking tall beers and the walls are like a log cabin and there's even a fireplace. Everyone seems shiny like lip gloss and I stare at the walls because my coat is cheap and I have a hole in my shoe. Plus there's no empty tables and I have no money and I don't speak Polish.

"Can I help you?" It's a girl holding red menus with white eagles on the front, which would have made a better family crest than the happy hot dog.

"I'm looking for my dad." I try to clench my teeth to stop them from knocking together but it doesn't work.

"Oh. Do you see him?"

"No. I mean, he's not here now." My cheeks are burning, which is weird next to my chattering teeth and I wonder if it would be crazier to stay here or run back to the bus stop.

"Oh. Was he . . . here earlier?"

"Um, yeah. I mean, not today. He used to be here, like, hang out here, before I was born. So I guess twelve years ago. I was just wondering if anybody remembered him." She opens her mouth to talk but before she can, I say really fast, "He used to sit and drink vodka with bison grass in it and he went to the University of Chicago and studied math and my mom was a waitress at the Irish pub across the street but it's not there anymore." Then I look down so I don't have to see her stare at me with perfect circle eyes (360 degrees).

She goes to talk to a waitress with long blond hair and black glasses that Marisol would laugh at but on her they look perfect. They talk about me and I pretend to look at a painting of a rooster on the wall like I've never seen a rooster before. Which I haven't. Not in real life anyway.

"Hey," the blond waitress says. She's younger than mom but older than high school so maybe in college because something about her seems smart. It might just be the glasses.

"Hey."

"You hungry?"

I'm starving. But I also feel like I might puke. "I don't have any money," I tell her. "I'm just looking for my dad. I mean, I'm just asking about him."

"I heard. What's his name?"

"Leszek Kowalski."

"And what's your name?"

"Brittany. Kowalski." My name sounds weird out

loud, like on the first day of school when everybody hears your name and then looks at you to see if it matches.

"Mine's Agata. Come on and sit up at the bar."

"Am I allowed?"

"Sure. I won't give you any *piwo.*" I blink at her. "That's beer." I smile a really huge smile like you give your kindergarten teacher but I don't care because I like her so much. I slide up onto a stool and the man next to me nods. Agata says something to the bartender and he makes me a drink with Sprite and cherry syrup and a skinny red straw and a real cherry floating on the top. It feels like heaven in this place. Maybe that's why people spend so much time at bars.

Agata rushes all around but she never looks rushed when she gets to the tables and I wonder if that's what makes a good waitress. If it is, Mom must have been the best waitress ever because she's so good at making her outside different than her inside. Thinking about her makes my stomach hurt and the cherry syrup doesn't help and neither does the thought that my dad could have sat on this same stool. I'm dizzy but I'm afraid to get down in case I fall over and make a scene. Or at least more of a scene than I've made so far.

Agata sets a huge plate of food in front of me that's still steaming. "Pierogi," she says, then leaves before I can ask what it is.

"You ever have ravioli?" the man next to me asks.

"Yeah."

"Kind of like ravioli," he says. "But better."

I want to tell Agata again that I have no money but she's back in the kitchen and the food smells so good so I just start eating. The dizziness stops. I don't know if it's the fire popping or the laughing or the tall stool or the cherry drink or the man next to me who smells like a grandpa in church or Agata moving like Mom or everything all together, but somehow the pierogis fill a hole that was way deeper than my stomach.

I eat every pierogi on the plate and I should probably be embarrassed (about a lot of things) but I'm not. I sit for a while not thinking about my dad

or anything but just feeling good. And sleepy. The tables get emptier and the man next to me leaves in a breeze of aftershave.

Agata sits down on his stool. "I asked around," she says. "About your dad. And your mom. I'm sorry to be the one to tell you this but twelve years is a long time."

"Yeah. I know." And I do. Whatever she's gonna say, I already know.

"The only person here back then was the cook and he doesn't remember. But I had him call his mother, Magda, because she knows everyone. You know those types?"

I think of Odessa and smile. "Yeah."

"Well, she also doesn't remember so it must be that he wasn't here that long." She looks at me and I can see how worried she is because her glasses make her eyes bigger. "I'm sorry," she says and I just stare at her because I can't believe she did all that for me. Plus the pierogis and the cherry Sprite. Mom was wrong about the Polish waitresses.

"Thanks for trying," I say.

Agata shrugs. "It's nothing."

And just like that, my dad is gone forever. And my Polish grandma and the Polish countryside where I could have seen my first real rooster.

Agata writes down my name and address just in case but I know it's over and I don't mind. I take a yellow coaster from the bar so I can glue it in my Plan B notebook. It's for a beer called Tatra and the picture has mountains and a huge, frosty mug of beer and a man in a black hat and brown vest holding a pipe and smiling. Maybe he looks just like my grandpa but I'll never know. I'm ready to go home. I want to see Mom.

eight

I'm playing with Tommy on the living room floor
hoping if I play with him enough he'll act like Mom
and me when he grows up instead of Jack. Mom's
on the couch reading every detail of my assignment notebook and all the different color pieces of
paper they send home on Mondays. The ones she
already read are stacked neatly beside her in a pile.
Granny's walking back and forth in the hall repeating something like "Twenty-six degrees down" but
Mom doesn't seem to notice.

I used to go to school without the field trip form

signed or wearing normal socks on crazy sock day or missing valentines. I used to complain to Mom and sometimes she would be gazing across the street or thinking about something funny Laila said and I would say, "Mom! Did you even hear me? I said the science fair poster was due TODAY!" But that never happens anymore because Jack made Mom so afraid to make a mistake. Now she reads every line, even about the school buses I don't ride.

Mom gasps when she finally makes it to the end of the stack. "Brittany!" she whispers. "Did you . . . make this?" She's holding up one of my cultural arts projects. This one worked a lot better than the happy hot dog. We were supposed to think of a person we love and draw how we feel when we're with them. "I don't want you to draw a picture of just the person," Mr. McInnis said. "I want you to draw the emotion." We groaned, of course, but not as much as we did during Kandinsky when he turned on the classical station and made us paint the music.

My hands started moving my markers like I wasn't controlling them, which was kind of scary but kind of cool. I was drawing Grandma Jane. I realized it when my hands were almost halfway done. It was Grandma and me holding hands in a park downtown and running to catch the ice cream truck bumbling along the park's edge. But it wasn't just that. It was the sunlight and the trees and the running to catch something we wanted and my small hand tight in hers and knowing she would never, ever, no matter what happened even if we lost the ice cream truck, let go.

"It's Grandma," Mom says.

"How'd you know?" I ask because the drawing really is an abstract.

"It's exactly how I used to feel with her," Mom says. Did I tell her the assignment? I don't think so. Maybe she read it in the stack of papers.

"How?" I ask.

"Powerful."

• • •

I have seven pages of information in my Plan B notebook but it's mostly drawings, and when I flip through it nothing pops out. No ideas and no plans.

Not even an outline of a plan, the way Mr. McInnis is teaching us to outline our five-paragraph essays before we write them. Most kids don't write five-paragraph essays until seventh grade but Mr. McInnis says we're old enough. He also says we'll never survive college if we don't know how to write a five-paragraph essay. None of us have the heart to tell him that none of us are going to college.

I shove the notebook back under the mattress and pull my coat on. Then I put Granny's coat on her too and lead her to the front door and undo all the locks. "I'm walking to the end of the block with Granny," I yell to Mom and shut the door behind us fast before she can say no. The air is cold but it feels good so maybe I just need to cool my brain off to think of a plan. We stand on the steps for a minute but I still don't think of a plan. "C'mon, Granny," I say and walk her to the sidewalk.

"Hey, you!" Odessa calls as we walk by. She's on her porch lifting the sheets off her plants, peeking at them like they're sleeping babies, whispering and smiling before covering them back up.

"Hey," I say back.

Odessa comes down her steps sideways, rocking back and forth a little. "This cold came on so quick!" she says. "I got the arthritis, so I feel it in my hips." She reaches the fence. "Oooh, girl!" she says really loud and I jump. "Don't ever get the arthritis!"

"I won't."

Odessa looks at Granny. "Not your granny, though. Look at her posture. Just perfect." I nod. Granny does stand up straight. Then Odessa lowers her voice to regular. "She thin, though, Lily," she says. "Thinner than I seen her before."

I look down at the ground. Somehow I feel like this is my fault. Probably 'cause I was off chasing a pretend Polish grandma when I should have been taking care of my real granny. "I know," I say. Granny starts to walk away. "See you later," I tell Odessa. We get to the end of the block and turn around before I realize Odessa called me Lily. I can't remember Granny ever calling me that in front of her and I want to ask her about it when we pass back by but she's already inside. The plants are all tucked in their pink and yellow beds and the porch light is off.

. . .

Mr. McInnis never said what happened at the principal's office but I guess not much because now he has a plan called Home Visits. "If your parents can't come to me," he says, "then I'll come to them. I'm going A to Z, so Ahmed Asan, I'll see you first!" Ahmed's the smallest kid in our class and he shrinks behind his desk and looks even smaller. Thinking about Home Visits gives everyone different faces so we look like a book Tommy has about feelings. My face is a mix of embarrassed and terrified. I have to think of a plan before Mr. McInnis gets to K.

"Kenya and Brittany," Mr. McInnis says. "Congratulations!" I hold my breath in case this announcement's even worse. "Our school has a new program that lets students with high reading scores go to the library once a week for free reading." Some of the kids laugh because this sounds like a punishment. I look at Kenya but her face is calm as always. We get our stuff and walk down the hall and into the library and sit down at desks next to each other before I realize I only brought my Plan B notebook.

I open it and try to flip to a new page without her noticing but she says, "What's that?" She's reading a book with a 9.2 on the spine which means she reads as good as a ninth grader.

"Nothing."

"Is it a journal?"

"Kind of."

"Cool."

Then I just tell her everything, about Jack and Mom and stealing the notebook from Dollar Tree and riding the bus to find my Polish grandma. I don't know why. Maybe it's because she's so quiet I know she won't tell anyone or maybe it's 'cause she said something about me is cool which no one has ever said in the history of the universe. "But I can't think of a plan," I tell Kenya. "I can't think of anything."

"My dad always says that to get to your future you have to look to your past."

"Oh. Is that like, an African proverb?"

"I don't think so. My dad's from Detroit." She pauses and I freeze because why did I have to say something so dumb right after she said I was cool? But then Kenya laughs. And once she starts she can't stop and I laugh too. We laugh and laugh. She's holding on to my arm and tears are in her eyes and I have to put my face on the desk I'm laughing so hard I can't sit up. I see the librarian lean over and I wait for her to shush us but she just grins.

• • •

After school I make a list in my Plan B notebook called To Get to Your Future You Have to Look to Your Past, and write all the memories I can think of. They start out nice like how the sun shined through a yellow tree and turned the glass gold at our old bus stop. But then I start thinking bad stuff like Mom getting mugged and our landlord eating cottage cheese and saying weird things. I write everything down because Kenya's dad didn't say Happy Past or Sad Past and my life is exactly like Mom said about the bag of trash and the bag of sea glass.

• • •

I'm sitting on the front stoop staring at the perfect blue sky and thinking about how strange November is, to be so cold and so pretty at the same time. The mail lady walks up and hands me the stack and it looks the same as always except for a huge pink envelope in the middle. I drop the rest of the mail pulling it out. "Your birthday card?" she asks. I shake my head. The card is to Daisy Hill but there's no return address.

"No," I say. "My great-grandma's."

"Is that right! How old is she now?"

"I don't know." I run up the steps and leave the rest of the mail scattered behind and bang through the door. Granny's sitting on the couch. She looks so pale and small. I haven't heard her mutter in days. Maybe she gave up trying to make us understand. I wonder what's inside her head, if she has words and pictures dancing around that can't get out or if it's a gray buzz like no radio station or just a silent snowy day.

"Granny," I say and sit down next to her. She doesn't turn or blink. She's so still I have to watch

her chest for a second to make sure she's breathing. She is. "Someone sent you a birthday card, I think." Nothing. "Can I open it?" Still nothing. I open it. A smiling pastel bumblebee covered in glitter is on the front, holding a magic wand with a star on top. It's a card for a little girl. Is that what's in Granny's head? Is she a little girl again?

The inside says, *Here's hoping all your wishes come true! Happy Birthday!* and someone wrote in shaky letters underneath, *Thinking of you. On your birthday and every day. Love, Fuzzy.* I read it out loud to Granny. "Who's Fuzzy?" I ask but she doesn't move. Mom and Jack are home. I can hear them picking up the mail. I shove the card and envelope between the couch cushions right before they walk in.

"Hey," Mom says. "How come the door's open and the mail's all over the front steps?"

"Sorry. I thought I heard Granny calling and I dropped it."

Jack looks at Granny who is a statue on the couch. I wait for him to shake the pizza ads at me

and say something ridiculous about identity theft (like anyone would want to be him) but he doesn't. He comes toward me and I freeze like Granny and he puts his hand on my head and tries to mess up my hair, but it doesn't work because I have a ponytail and also because I hate him. Mom is grinning like after I blow out the candles on my birthday cake and we all pretend whatever I wished for will come true.

"Just be more careful," Jack says. I nod and glance at Granny. She has flower-shop eyes and the corners of her mouth twitch, just a little, and I know she is thinking of Fuzzy.

• • •

The cops don't come to our school like they go to the high school but when they do it's usually to the lunchroom. Today two kids got in a fistfight and some other kids turned it into a food fight and now five of them are in handcuffs, sitting on the floor with all the smashed hamburgers and ketchup. One of them actually has a French fry stuck to his shoulder.

Mr. McInnis is standing at the end of the row with his glasses off, rubbing his eyebrows, because two of the five are in my class. One is Ladarius Prince, who's always in trouble and is right now shaking his head at the cops and smiling. But the other is Jerome Hawkins, huge and smart and silent and wouldn't hurt a fly. His head is down. That's the one Mr. McInnis is rubbing his eyebrows about.

Marisol is holding Granny's card open in front of her so the bumblebee is smiling and glittering at me, waving its magic wand over my cold hamburger. "Maybe he's a secret admirer," she says.

"Are you serious? She never goes out. And she's old. It has to be someone from a long time ago."

Marisol shrugs. "A secret admirer from a long time ago, then. 'On your birthday and every day!' That's not just a friend. It's either a secret admirer or family. That's what I say." She sets the card down and chews on a fry. "These are disgusting." Over her shoulder, the five boys struggle to their feet without using their hands, except Jerome. He stands up straight as an arrow. Mr. McInnis leans toward him to say something.

"How am I ever gonna find him? I don't know his real name. I don't know his last name. I don't even know where he lives. What am I gonna do? Walk around the rest of my life calling for Fuzzy?"

Marisol lays the next fry in a pool of ketchup and rolls it back and forth. "Why do you need to find him anyways? First your dad and now Fuzzy. What are you looking for? Hate to break it to you, girl, but this"—she spreads her hands out like the dim cafeteria and the cold food and the hard shouts are the showcase in an old game show—"is your life."

The boys are gone but the blue lights still flash through the windows. Mr. McInnis is standing at the side door with his hands in his pockets, looking out. I can't decide if Marisol is right or wrong but I think both. "I know," I tell her. The bell rings and Mr. McInnis startles like Mom does sometimes. He turns and walks toward the steps, back to the hallway and the classroom and the other thirty of us. "I just think maybe he can . . . help."

Marisol gives me a smile like you give a little kid who can't hit a baseball. "But you do know where he lives," she says.

"What do you mean?"

Marisol taps her finger on an ink circle on the pink envelope. She hasn't stopped biting her nails. Her mom paints that nasty stuff on them but Marisol just chews through it. "Ever heard of a post-mark?"

• • •

Every night since Fuzzy's card came I can't sleep. I close my eyes but all I see is the pink envelope the way you can still see the sun through your eyelids at the beach. Mom always sent me to the lake in a sun hat but Grandma Jane didn't make me wear it because she said it was a special thing to feel your hair in the wind and see it afterward in the mirror all full of sand and water and tangles and sunshine.

I try to see Montgomery, Alabama, the city spelled out where Marisol tapped her finger, but I don't know what to picture besides cotton so I just make up stories about the ceiling stains above my bed or see how fast I can run my eyes along the window bars or stare at all the art we've made this year that already covers half my wall. It's more art than we did in all of fourth grade. Maybe all of third and fourth put together.

Then I pull out my Plan B notebook and turn to a blank page so Mom won't see the cover. Tommy and Granny are asleep and Jack's out and Mom's washing dishes at the kitchen sink under weak light. I sit down at the table and she jumps. "Oh. Hey, Brit. What's the matter? Can't sleep?"

"No, I just forgot about this assignment I was supposed to start," I lie. "It's a profile of Granny."

"Mmm. Okay." She turns back to the sink and I watch her for a minute. She's not in a hurry to finish the dishes. She lets her hands rest in the soapy water with each dish before lifting and rinsing and setting it careful to dry.

"So Granny's husband was Frank Hill?"

"Yes. Well, no. Frank's last name was something else. Granny kept her maiden name. I don't know why. Grandma always said it was very unusual dur-

ing those days. Women never kept their names, or used dashes or anything." Mom shrugs. "I guess she just wanted to stay Daisy Hill."

I write this down. "Now I need her brothers and sisters," I tell Mom.

"Whose?"

"Granny's."

"Seriously?"

"Mom! It's for school!"

"I know, I know. It's fine, Brit. It's just so . . . detailed."

"Well, that's how Mr. McInnis is." Mom turns from her soapy sink to smile at me and I remember in that instant how much I love her. I look down at my notebook. "So what were their names?"

Mom sucks in air through her teeth and for a second I think she cut her hand on a knife but then I realize she just really wants to have the answers. "She had three sisters, I think. No, four. No, three. There were four girls. I don't remember their names, baby, I'm sorry. Granny was somewhere in the middle. And there was one brother but I don't know his real name. It started with an *H*. Harold or Harvey? I'm sorry, Brit, this isn't very helpful."

"It's okay. What do you mean you don't know his real name?"

"Well, we just called him Uncle Fuzzy."

I hop up from the table. "Okay, well, that's a good start. Thanks, Mom."

Mom sets down the dish she's holding and stares at me. "Is that all you need?" she asks.

"Yeah, we can finish tomorrow. I'm pretty tired, so." I actually fake a yawn.

"Brittany?" Mom asks as I turn to go.

"Yeah?"

"I'm sorry I can't tell you anything about your dad's side."

"It's okay."

She nods and smiles with half her mouth like the other half couldn't decide what to do.

nine

Jerome hasn't been back since the lunchroom fight.
Some kids say he's locked up and some say he's living at the shelter on Roosevelt and some say his grandma put him on a bus to Baltimore to live with his dad. Some kids say his mom's a crackhead and that's why Jerome is slow. But I've sat behind him all year and I've seen his papers. He gets straight As. Which is not easy in Mr. McInnis's class. He's not like other teachers who pass us along like that game we used to play in first grade. Hot potato.

Mr. McInnis is distracted. On Tuesday he kept

saying Van Gogh when he meant Gauguin. On Wednesday he forgot how to multiply fractions. And yesterday he just gave up at 2:35, turned off all the lights, and told us to think about what we're thankful for in preparation for Thanksgiving, which is six days away. I don't want to bother him but if I don't I'll have to spend the whole weekend with no way to work on Plan B. Fuzzy's the best lead I have. Fuzzy is the only lead.

When everyone goes to recess, I wait behind. "Need something, Brittany?" Mr. McInnis asks. His voice sounds like someone recorded it and played it back from far away.

"Um, yeah. Only if you have time. I just need help with something. But it's not for school. It's . . . for something else." Mr. McInnis nods. "I need to find a Fuzzy Hill in Alabama. In Montgomery, actually." Mr. McInnis stares at me with ragged-quilt eyes.

"Sorry! That sounded weird. Fuzzy Hill's a person. I just need help looking up his phone number."

Mr. McInnis crosses his arms. "Who is he?" he asks.

"He's my great-grandma's brother. He sent her a birthday card and she wants to call him to thank him I guess. But my mom doesn't have his number and we don't have a computer and I thought maybe you could help me look it up here. But it's no big deal, really." I start to back away. I've never lied to Mr. McInnis and it feels worse than stealing the Plan B notebook. If Mr. McInnis knew, would he wink at me like the girl with wedding cake hair? Somehow I don't think so. I just want to go to recess.

"No, no. It's fine," Mr. McInnis says, standing up. "I'll help you. Let's go down to the lab." We walk down the hall and my stomach is dancing around in my throat but I don't know if it's because it's just Mr. McInnis and me in the hall or because I just lied to him. "Do you know his real first name?" he asks.

"No. But I know it starts with an H."

"Okay, well. We can try that." He pushes the computer lab door and holds it open so I go first. There are a few kids inside and none of them look up. We sit down and Mr. McInnis pulls up a map of the United States on the screen and zooms in on the South. "Do you know where Montgomery is?" he asks. I shake my head. He points to Alabama, the green state. To the star in the middle.

"So, Alabama's next to Mississippi," I say, pointing to the pink state to the left. "Where you're from."

He smiles. "Yes, ma'am," he says and somehow sounds just like Odessa even though they are exact opposites.

"Are you from their capital?" I squint so I can read it. "From Jackson?"

Mr. McInnis laughs. "No, I'm from the opposite. The closest thing on the map to where I'm from are the Palestinian Gardens. It's a scaled model of Palestine as it was when Jesus walked the earth, built from concrete blocks and car headlights all covered in white plaster. One Mississippi yard equals one Palestinian mile."

"Oh."

Then Mr. McInnis pulls up a list of every H. Hill in Montgomery. There are fifty-two. "Looks like you've got your work cut out for you," he says. He

clicks print and types in his code and I watch his balance drop from $1.10 to $0.30.

"I'll bring you eighty cents on Monday," I promise when he hands me the papers.

He shakes his head. "No need. Just glad I could help." I pull the door open to go to recess and through the swooshing shut I hear him add, "For once."

• • •

Laila heard about a church giving away food for Thanksgiving so we're all on the Madison bus. I'm in the very front seat next to Miles and our moms are behind us. Mom's jiggling Tommy, who's crying, and Laila's making faces at him, which is making him cry louder. You can see downtown all the way from here, filling up the windshield, and we're making our way toward it, block by block, stopping and waiting and starting.

I keep my eyes on the Willis Tower. Grandma Jane took me to the top of it when it was still the Sears and we could see the whole city with the people like bugs and the boats like turtles in the lake and Grandma said, "See how big the world is?" I was small but I wasn't afraid. My hands were sweaty and my bangs were in my eyes. A man stepped in front of me and Grandma lifted me up so I could still see. "Don't ever forget that," she said. Mom says I never went to the Willis Tower when it was still the Sears but I remember Grandma's face, sunny from the bright glass.

We don't make it to the Willis Tower today. Mom squeezes my shoulder when we're still very far away and says, "This is us." The trees are still scrawny and the buildings are still worn out and I think, *Yeah, this is us.* I climb down the steps holding Miles's hand and watch the bus chug away. The faces pass by one by one and I wonder if any of them will make it all the way downtown and up all the elevator floors to the very top of the tower where the world is so big. Probably not.

At the church, Laila and Mom each get a small frozen turkey and a paper bag filled with mixes for cornbread, stuffing, and mashed potatoes, and cans of corn and green beans and cranberries. There's also a four-pack of chocolate pudding for dessert. Mom and Laila thank the ladies passing out the food and we leave the church through the side door. Mom's carrying Tommy in one arm and the bag in the other so I carry the turkey, which is heavy, but I don't mind because the bag makes me so sad.

Because Thanksgiving's not supposed to come from a brown bag at a brown church. It's supposed to be different. I don't know how, but it is. Like the difference between our neighborhood with its bare houses and stale streets and the Willis Tower, surrounded by turquoise water and shiny stores and huge trees with red and yellow leaves. We cross the street to the bus stop on the other side and wait in the cold wind, which I use to explain my tears, the way Mom does.

• • •

Marisol got me a phone for fifteen minutes. She bribed Tonio to use his cell by threatening to tell their mom that he skipped school and went downtown with Estella all day Friday. When Mom takes Granny and Tommy down the block for some fresh air, I tear a page from my Plan B notebook, scribble a note on it, and run all the way to Marisol's.

Tonio hands me the phone. "Who you callin', anyway?" he asks. "Your boyfriend?"

"None of your business!" Marisol tells him and slams her bedroom door. Tonio's as mild as a glass of milk, so Marisol can say anything to him. Before she slammed the door in his face, Tonio raised both hands like surrendering and turned away laughing and shaking his head. I start to think about what Jack would do if I said *None of your business!* and slammed a door but stop because I try never to think about Jack.

I dial the first H. Hill on the list. A woman answers and I ask for Fuzzy. "Sorry, doll," she says. "You have the wrong number." I cross it off. No one picks up at the next H. Hill, or the one after that. The fourth H. Hill has an answering machine that says Buddy and Sudie live there so I cross it off. Why was that an *H* anyway? A boy answers at the next one. "Who?" he asks. I repeat Fuzzy's name. "Naw," he says. "No Fuzzy here." And on and on. Some of the numbers I cross off but so many just ring. I'm only halfway through the list and I've already used up eight minutes. I call the next one.

"No, Fuzzy doesn't live here," she says. "Who's calling, please?"

"Um, Brittany?" I tell her. "My great-grandma is Fuzzy's sister."

"And who is your great-grandmother, dear?"

"Daisy Hill."

"Oh, for goodness' sakes. How is that sweet lady?"

"Um, she's fine, I guess. Kind of quiet."

"But still livin'. God bless her, she always did know how to set out in the sunshine and turn her face up. You want to take down Fuzzy's number?"

"Yeah! I mean, thank you, yes."

She tells it to me and I can barely write the numbers my hands are shaking so bad. Marisol's jumping up and down and pumping her fists to the sky. I can feel the buzzing all over my body again, like when I made Mr. McInnis laugh. I thank her, hang up, and dial Fuzzy's number before I can chicken out. It rings three times, and halfway through the fourth, a man answers. "Hello?"

"Hi, Fuzzy?"

"Yes, speaking."

"Hi, you don't know me but my name's Brittany and I'm Daisy Hill's great-granddaughter? She lives with us now. We got your birthday card. I mean, she did. I read it to her. Anyway."

Tonio knocks on the door. Marisol goes to talk him into a few more minutes but Estella's there and she's ready to go.

"Well, hey, darlin'," Fuzzy says in a voice that takes its time. "It's so nice to hear from you. How's Daisy doin'? I think about her every day."

Estella marches across Marisol's bedroom, holds her hand out to me, and shoots her eyebrows as high as they can go. She's wearing a man's tank top that's supposed to go under a shirt and it's turquoise and I try not to stare at the black lace of her bra

underneath or think about if she's wearing underwear.

"She's fine," I tell Fuzzy. My voice sounds squeaky
and Estella rolls her eyes. "Um, Fuzzy? I'll call you
back, okay?"

Estella grabs the phone and pushes the red but-
ton with one perfectly curved tangerine fingernail.
"Sorry," she says in a voice that's not sorry. "Time's
up. You'll have to talk to your Fuzzy friend later."
But her eyes aren't mean like she pretends to be.
They're left behind.

• • •

We're watching the parade on TV and eating Pills-
bury cinnamon rolls because that's what Mom used
to do on Thanksgiving morning when she was little. But Jack is here so we're all sitting up straight
and not talking like Granny. We're also shivering
because Jack says Mom uses too much heat and
turned it down. And the cinnamon rolls aren't right.
They taste like metal, like the dentist's office, like
being afraid. I don't want to eat them but my body's

so hungry and so cold I can't stop. I already had two and I want another one but there are only eight, and three-eighths is almost half, so.

Tommy crawls into my bedroom and Mom stands up to get him but I say, "It's okay. He can play in there," and follow him. He crawls all the way to the other side of the bed and pulls on the covers. I lie across the bed and play peep-eye with him, which is what Grandma Jane called peekaboo. He likes it. "Thanks, Tommy," I whisper because he got us away from Jack and the metal rolls and all the smiling balloons and pretty hair singers and kids in perfectly round red mittens. The announcers keep saying how cold it is in New York this morning but nobody looks cold.

I give Tommy the hair ribbons Marisol gave me and he chews on them with his two teeth while I make a list in my Plan B notebook.

Questions for Fuzzy

1. Is there winter in Alabama?

2. Why did Granny keep her maiden name and was her husband (Frank) mad?
3. Where did Granny live before she lived with us?
4. Who is Lily?

. . .

It's the last night of the brown-bag Thanksgiving, which I ended up thankful for because it's been the one warm thing in all the cold days. Granny's coughing and Tommy got so tired Mom put him to bed early and Jack's been gone for hours but Mom still won't turn the heat up. "He's coming back," she says. "Trust me."

"Yeah right," I say and fill the tub up as high as it can go with the hottest water I can stand. Mom doesn't stop me so water must be cheaper than gas. But it gets cold eventually.

Granny's already in bed when I get out with my chin trembling like right before you cry. I put on my warmest clothes and slide in next to her. She's so thin I'm worried she won't have enough body heat to make it through the night but she doesn't shiver like me. She's perfectly still.

We're on our backs with our elbows touching looking up and I wonder if somewhere in a warm place like Alabama there's another Granny and another Brittany lying side by side in sleeping bags looking up at the stars and smelling a campfire and tasting marshmallows and graham crackers in their throats and the Granny is telling old stories and the Brittany is just listening and wiggling her toes in her wool socks.

I look at Granny and her face is pale and her mouth is open a little and her eyes are windows washed. "It's okay, Granny," I whisper. "I know you'd tell me your stories if you could." Then it's like a barrel of sleep tips over on me. I feel Mom lay another blanket on us and I want to tell her it's not enough and she has to do better but I'm just too tired.

Then the front doorknob is jiggling. Jack's voice comes in and out and up and down like he's riding a roller coaster in the living room, but Mom's is steady and quiet. The TV comes on and Mom is in the kitchen popping a beer and I guess I don't understand beer because I thought if you wanted someone to be nicer you wouldn't give them more of it.

I breathe in and out, matching my breath to Tommy's, fast, then Granny's, slow. My hair is cold. I try to fall back asleep but I'm wide awake. After a long time the TV hisses off and the hall light flashes to nothing and maybe in a crazy way Mom knows what she's doing.

ten

I'm so happy to be back at school I can't stop smiling. It's so warm here. I am thinking thoughts again. I am thinking lots and lots of thoughts, like my brain's trying to catch up after four days of being frozen. I can barely sit still. I want to draw a picture and write a book and solve the hardest math problem at the same time. I also want to take a nap. Even though you barely move, being cold is very tiring.

Mr. McInnis is excited too. He's standing in front of the class with the book about Ivan the gorilla we were all supposed to read. He set page goals for every week starting in September. He reminded us every day that we had to finish by Thanksgiving. I'm glad I didn't wait till the last minute because my brain would've been too cold. "Okay," Mr. McInnis says. "Now I want an honest show of hands. I won't be mad. How many of you read any of the book? It's okay if you didn't finish it. Remember, honesty."

Five of us raise our hands. Five out of thirty-two. Well, five out of thirty because one kid's absent and Jerome is still gone. That's exactly one-sixth, so at least I'm learning to reduce fractions. I want to tell Mr. McInnis this but I don't think it will help. He's still looking around at the hands, waiting for more to go up. "Okay!" he finally announces too loud, like trying to convince himself that it really is okay. "No problem!" he adds. He has the five of us form a circle in the back to discuss the themes of the book and tells the other kids to read the first ten pages.

• • •

It's been one month since we went to WIC and we're back at WIC. But now it's winter so everyone's coughing. Mom holds Tommy tight like she can protect him from all the germs sailing around the room like bad magic carpets. Even worse, WIC got a grubby train table so now all the not-sick kids are running around pelting each other with boxcars while the sick kids watch from their moms' laps, sniffing their snot back up or just letting it run down. I'm hungry and out of homework so I lean my head on Mom's shoulder even though it's bony and not comfortable at all. Her hair smells nice.

This time it's Faiza who gives us the vouchers. She's my favorite because she doesn't say the thing about breastfeeding that makes Mom look at the floor, and when she asks which baby foods Tommy has tried and how much formula he drinks she looks at Mom and not at the computer and she always has teddy bear eyes. Today she's even wearing a fuzzy brown sweater so it's easy to picture her as a teddy bear with a teddy bear husband and two cute (but wild) teddy bear boys. Probably it's not normal to think this stuff and I wonder if being hungry is starting to make me nuts.

Then Faiza reads my mind. "What about your daughter?" she says and turns into a person again.

"What do you mean?" Mom asks but in an easy voice because she likes Faiza too. "She's too old for WIC, isn't she?"

Faiza's laugh is twinkly like the little flying fairies in Sleeping Beauty. I wonder if she'd be the red or blue or green one. Do fairies get to choose? "She is, yes, but how is her eating?"

Mom looks at me. "She's a good eater. She'll try anything."

"That's good, that's good." Faiza smiles at me. "Good to try new things!" I smile back. But then she talks quieter.

"But I mean, is she getting enough? She's growing fast now and she'll need more calories for her body and brain to develop strong and healthy."

"Oh," Mom says, and all of a sudden I'm scared my stomach will growl and betray Mom. I hold my breath.

"You get the SNAP benefits?" Faiza asks, and Mom nods. She doesn't tell her that plenty of times

Jack steals her card and somehow uses it for cigarettes.

But unlike the mean WIC lady, Faiza knows when to stop. "Good," she says and I turn her back into a teddy bear, just for a second. "Lots of fruits and vegetables, and mostly vegetables!" she tells me, with the fairy laugh. "And some nuts or fish for protein."

I make my face into *Very interesting!* and nod like I can follow her advice. I wish she would ask what Mom eats, which is almost nothing, but our time is up.

• • •

I turn my Plan B notebook sideways so I can draw Faiza's vegetables like Cézanne painted fruit. Mr. McInnis told us Cézanne's dad wanted him to be a lawyer or at least work in the family bank but he kept painting instead and made over two hundred still lifes, not to mention the landscapes and portraits, so I guess that showed him. Also Cézanne made objects *significant* by using *intense color* so I push hard on my markers since some of them are drying up. But nothing really looks significant, except maybe the eggplant, but that's probably because it's so purple.

Mom used to grow vegetables every summer in big pots on the fire escape. The green beans grew right up the railings to the fourth floor. Before Grandma Jane left every September she'd pick everything and put it in mason jars and it would last almost until she came back. We could really use those jars now. Except Grandma didn't think vegetables had to be healthy like Faiza because whenever we bought *elotes* from the street carts she'd get butter and mayonnaise and parmesan and salt and black pepper and red pepper so you could barely see the corn underneath.

"Mom says all that's bad for you," I told her once and Grandma said, "Your mama, she's so good. Just like her daddy, rest his soul. But sometimes, peanut"—and she leaned down so our faces were in the shade of her big floppy straw hat—"you just gotta *live*!"

• • •

Marisol didn't have to bribe Tonio to use his phone this time because Estella broke up with him for a boy with a car that rides so low it scrapes the ground when it goes over bumps. Marisol says it has a leather interior but I don't see why that's more important than having a boyfriend who's nice. Marisol says I'll understand someday. All Tonio does now is sit on the couch and watch *Simpsons* reruns because he says if he doesn't laugh he'll cry. I want to punch Estella in the face. When we take Tonio's phone from the couch he doesn't even flinch.

This time Fuzzy answers on the second ring but skips the first part of hello and just says, "'Lo."

"Hi, Fuzzy? It's Brittany again, Daisy's great-granddaughter? Sorry it took me so long to call you back but it's hard for me to get a phone." I'm holding the phone between Marisol and me because she wants to listen.

"Well, hey, sugar. I was hopin' you'd call me back someday." His voice reminds me of the music those foreign guys played that made Granny walk down the block.

I look at my notebook. "Um. I was wondering if you could answer some questions for me? It's for a project, for school."

"Well, I don't know but I'll sure do my best," he says. The way he talks makes my chest hurt and also makes me want to sleep on his couch forever. I don't care if it's old and scratchy and smells like medicine. I don't even care if I have a blanket.

"Okay. The first one is . . ." I skip the one about winter in Alabama because it doesn't seem important. "Why did Granny keep her maiden name and was her husband, Frank, mad?"

Fuzzy chuckles. "You know, I never did ask her why. But your granny always has had her own mind. I guess she felt like her name was how she liked it. And Frank was the nicest man you'd ever hope to meet. He was so in love with your granny he wouldn't care if she changed her name to Giddyap and dyed her hair purple." I think of Tonio and smile.

"Okay, thanks. The next one is, where did Granny live before she lived with us?"

"Well, she lived in her house. Right down the road from me. Lived there"—Fuzzy makes a whistling sound in his teeth—"gosh, fifty years, I guess. You were there when you were just a tiny thing. I know you don't remember." He chuckles again. "Time does pass."

"Her house?" I ask. "Who lives there now?" My heart thumps in my whole body like the bass from the cars at sunset.

"Nobody does," Fuzzy says. "I been tryin' to keep it up some. You know, runnin' the water when we get a freeze and standin' the windows open once in a while. I cut the grass in the summertime. Don't have but a little patch."

My brain's like a speeding train now and I can't focus. I know I should ask something else about the house but I don't know what. It's too weird to ask if we can live there. Marisol writes in huge capital letters on the bottom of the page and holds it up: *RENT.*

"Who pays the rent?" I ask Fuzzy. I know it's the

biggest bill because it's the one Mom worries about the most.

"You sure are sharp for a girl your age," Fuzzy tells me. "How old are you now, Miss Brittany?"

"Eleven."

Fuzzy whistles in his teeth again. "That house been paid for a long time, honey. Nobody has to pay the rent."

Marisol and I stare at each other. She shakes her head a little and her earrings clink. I don't know what else to say so I say, "Thanks for all your help, Fuzzy. I gotta go now but I'll call you again really soon."

"Brittany? Before you go, hon. How's your mama?"

"She's okay."

"Well, you just tell her I said hello, and if there's anything she needs for Daisy . . . or for anybody, just call."

"I will. Thanks, Fuzzy. I'll call you again soon. I promise."

. . .

Sundays are the worst because my homework's always done and the library's closed. And today's worse than most Sundays because I don't know what to do next in my Plan B. I just stare out the window and see whatever comes by, which isn't much. Granny's next to me with her head leaned back against the couch, sleeping quiet as a mouse. I hold her hand because she doesn't let me when she's awake. She wiggles away if you try to hold on to her at all.

I'm wondering if I could make it to the lowest branch of the tree across the street from Odessa's and what I'd do when I got there, when a long white car pulls up and parks underneath it. After a minute, Tiny gets out. He opens the back door and leans in and he's so huge he fills up the whole space.

When he comes back out he's holding a baby in a puffy pink snowsuit and a pink diaper bag over his shoulder. He leans back into the car and finds her hat and puts it on her head. He's smiling and talking silly to her like we do to Tommy. I can't hear him but I can just tell. He sees me in the window and I smile. He waves and I wave back.

"Who are you waving to?" Mom is suddenly next to me holding Tommy and her voice came out so sharp Granny's eyes pop awake and move back and forth between us like she's trying to decide if we're her family or not.

"Tiny," I tell Mom.

"How do you know him?"

"He's Odessa's nephew."

"But how do you know him?" She's jiggling Tommy even though he's not fussing.

"He brought you Gatorade when you were sick."

"Did he?" Mom's still looking out the window even though Tiny's already inside.

"Yeah. Did you know he was a preemie and he could fit in his daddy's hand and no one thought he would make it?" Mom just looks at me. Probably the way I looked at Odessa when she told me. It *is* hard to believe.

Mom sighs and I say, "What?"

"You're just . . ."

"What?" I ask in a half-mad voice because I didn't do anything wrong and neither did Tiny and why doesn't she appreciate the Gatorade?

"Getting older."

This makes no sense. If this was dialogue in a story, Mr. McInnis would say it has no *flow*. I think about telling Mom this but instead I say, "I'm gonna draw for a while," and go into my room and shut the door. I pull out my Plan B notebook and draw a picture of Tiny that fills up the whole page with his baby as a little pink puffball in his arms and underneath it I write exactly what Odessa told me so I don't forget. *You don't ever know what a person will grow up to be. You just got to wait and see. People do surprise you.*

eleven

Mr. McInnis told Ms. Sanogo he's given up on
getting any more of us to read about Ivan, especially
at home where things are *complicated.* Now we're
doing state reports *in class* and he let us choose
any state we wanted. Eleven kids had to put their
name in a baggie for Illinois, which reminded me
of Grandma Jane saying the world is so big, but no
one in my class seems to know it. Nobody wanted
Alabama but me. Nobody wanted Mississippi either
until Mr. McInnis realized Leon and Sofía both had

New York and assigned Mississippi to Sofía. She wasn't happy about it and neither was Mr. McInnis.

We're on the Madison bus again but this time I'm not looking at the Willis Tower and the way the spikes reach into the white sky like they could reach anything. Today I'm drawing everything Alabama. I finished the yellowhammer and the camellia and the longleaf pine and now I'm bent over the eastern tiger swallowtail butterfly, which is hard to do because its spots are like watercolors that dripped down its back. The light is fading outside and I have to lift my paper closer to the window.

"Is that about Alabama?" Mom asks.

"Yeah. It's for school," I tell her and it's nice that it's not a lie. "We're doing state reports."

"And you got Alabama?"

"No. I chose it."

Mom smiles a wide grin that I forgot she had. "Grandma would be so pleased," she says.

"Yeah."

She looks down at Tommy, half sleeping and half pulling on her necklace, then out the front of the

bus toward the Willis Tower, which is almost buried in winter fog. But she doesn't see it anyway. Her eyes are swimming in the sea. I wonder if Grandma ever took her up to the top when it was still the Sears and told her the world is so big. If she did, Mom forgot.

• • •

At Walgreens they don't have Granny's medicine ready even though the doctor said they would call it in. Mom has to stand at the counter while a lady with earrings that almost touch her shoulders calls the doctor's office and waits for them to call back and she's so tired she says yes when I ask if I can go to aisle 9 to look at magazines.

I sit down on the floor and flip through one of the magazines Marisol likes, full of boys with messy hair and guitars and sunglasses with gold rims. But they seem so far away, like the people in the Thanksgiving parade. I can feel in my bones that none of them ever sat on a bright and dirty Walgreens floor at eight o'clock on a school night waiting for medicine to help their granny think and for some reason it makes me so mad. I shove the magazine back on the rack and don't care that I wrinkled it.

I stand up to go back to Mom and the lady with the huge hoops but then I notice the maps. Most of them are for Chicagoland, which is a trick because it makes the city sound like a fairy tale (which it's not) but there's an atlas with a map of all fifty states on the first page, covered in blue highways like veins. It's not the way I want to think about our country. I want to think about it like *from the red-wood forests to the gulf-stream waters.* But I find Chicago anyway, then I find Alabama and run my finger between them through Indiana, Kentucky, and Tennessee.

It's a long way to Montgomery.

• • •

After school it's my favorite kind of snow. The quiet kind that falls super slow so you don't have to worry about not having a shovel for the steps or if the buses will be on time. Mom's wearing her bright orange and yellow scarf that looks like a sunbeam in winter. Grandma Jane knit it for her when she moved to Chicago but she'd never knit a scarf before and it's about ten feet long. Mom doesn't care. She just wraps it around and around. She pulls it down to smile at me. This kind of snow makes everyone happy. That's the other reason it's my favorite.

"How was school?" Mom asks. We start walking in no hurry, like the snow. Tommy's grabbing at the flakes with his little pink hands.

"Good. Marco brought his pet turtle and it got loose and Dahlia jumped on her desk screaming because she says once her uncle got salmonella from a turtle and almost died."

"Wow." Mom smiles. "Guess what I got at the store today? That kind of hot chocolate you like, you know, with the little marshmallows?"

"Yes!" I say because I really do love those little marshmallows. "Why'd you get it?"

"Just felt like we needed it."

We walk along and I think about Granny's empty house in Montgomery because I can't stop thinking about it. "Mom?" I ask. "What kind of job would

you want if you could have one? I mean, did you like being a waitress?"

"It was all right," Mom says. "But if I could have any job, I think I'd like to work in a bank. As a teller. You know, the people at the counter who count out the money?"

"Yeah. You're really good with money," I tell her and it's true. Every week when we go to the store, the card gets so close to zero but it never goes under. Never. Except when Jack messes with it but that's not Mom's fault.

"I'd be better at it if I had a little more," Mom says, and her laugh ends halfway through like it decided it probably wasn't that funny. But I'm smiling because I know there are banks everywhere. I know there are banks in Montgomery.

• • •

Kenya's house looks a lot like mine. I didn't know she lived so close until Mr. McInnis set a huge stack of papers on my desk and said, "Would you mind dropping this off at Kenya's? She's still sick and her dad called asking for her homework." I told him

I didn't know where she lived and he said, "She's right around the corner from you!" and I blushed because Mr. McInnis knows where I live even though Mr. McInnis knows where everyone lives because of Home Visits. He's already at *F*.

I lift the front of Tommy's stroller while Mom and I walk up the steps. The porch is clean and empty except for a welcome mat in the shape of a pineapple. I ring the doorbell and Tommy kicks his feet which makes his boots fall off so I'm bent down pushing them back on when the door opens and Kenya's dad smiles at me. He's in a wheelchair so we're face to face and there are little plastic tubes going from his nose around his ears to a big tank on wheels.

I just stare at him because he's not who I pictured saying *school board* and *policy* and *To get to your future you have to look to your past* and then I feel terrible for thinking that because why couldn't he be? Mom nudges me at the same moment Kenya's dad says, "Hi there," and his voice booms like a storm in July. The kind Mom and I used to listen to in the tiny apartment on the third floor where we lived before Jack. Mom used to turn off all the lights so we could see the lightning better. Lots of kids are scared of thunder but I'm not.

I stand up. "Hi. Um, my name's Brittany. I'm in Mr. McInnis's class with Kenya? I brought her homework." I hold out the stack and he takes it and sets it on his lap.

"Thank you, Brittany. And—?" He looks at Mom and she smiles.

"Maureen," she says and shakes his hand because she always knows what to do in these kinds of situations.

"Maureen! I haven't heard that name in a long time. How beautiful."

"Thank you," Mom says.

"I surely appreciate this. Kenya was starting to worry about falling behind."

"She doesn't need to worry," I tell him. "She's one of the smartest kids in our class."

"Is that so?"

I nod.

"She says you're pretty smart yourself. Says you've got a plan." I can feel Mom looking at me but I don't look back. "I'd invite you in but you don't want that child's cough." He shakes his head and I notice how old he looks, more like a grandpa than a dad. "I guess I'd better let you go before you freeze to death." He pushes his wheels and his chair rolls back a little. "Thanks again!"

"No problem at all," Mom says. "I hope she feels better." The door shuts and we carry Tommy's stroller back down the steps and out the gate. "What'd he mean by that?" Mom asks.

"By what?"

"That you've got a plan."

"I don't know. He probably says that to everyone."

Mom holds on to my arm before I can walk ahead of her and bends down and kisses me right on the forehead.

• • •

Mom made chicken and dumplings for dinner, Granny's favorite, but Granny won't eat a bite. It might be because it's mostly dumplings and not so much chicken but I don't say anything because Mom's arm is stiff like a robot when she lifts the spoon to Granny, talking to her in the same voice she used to get Tommy to eat his baby food before he started shoveling Cheerios in his mouth. Maybe if Mom tried flying the spoon like an airplane. I laugh out loud, I don't mean to, and Mom gives me spiky-leaf eyes. "Sorry," I say. "I was laughing at Tommy."

Tommy squeezes a dumpling in his fist and smears it on his tray. "Bee bee bee," he tells us, then rubs his hand in his hair. Mom doesn't even smile. She sets Granny's spoon down and goes to the kitchen sink and just stares out the window into the winter black. I pull Granny's bowl closer and lift the spoon toward her but she hardly seems real. Her skin's almost white and her eyes are tipped up. "Here, Granny," I say and hold the spoon closer but she doesn't move. It's like trying to feed a ghost. Tommy leans way over in his chair and sticks out his tongue but this time I don't laugh.

．．．

At school we each have to pick one of the seven principles of Kwanzaa and write about what it means in our lives. Most of the kids are squinting at the list of African words and trying to remember what Mr. McInnis said about them but I know exactly which one I'm doing. *Kujichagulia.* Self-determination. *To define ourselves, name ourselves, create for ourselves, and speak for ourselves.* I pick the sharpest pencil out of my desk.

<u>Kujichagulia</u>. Self-determination. To me this means doing what you want and not what anyone else wants you to do. But this is hard when you're a kid because you don't get to make the big decisions that determine things. Like I can decide who my best friend is (Marisol) or what my favorite color is (yellow) but I can't decide to never see Jack again or live in a different part of the city or keep Patches. I didn't name myself and I can't really speak for myself unless I want to get in trouble. I guess I define

myself (kind of) and create for myself but it doesn't seem to do any good.

If I could speak for myself, I would tell Jack I hate him. I would tell Mom that she is pretty and strong like pansies in the snow. I would tell Tommy that I will always take care of him (and he would understand me). I would tell Granny that I will find her home and take her there someday (and she would understand me). I would tell Marisol she's smart enough to have a real job and I would tell my class the world is so big. And I would tell myself

The bell rings, which is good, because I can't think of one thing to tell myself.

twelve

Laila's waiting for me after school instead of Mom.
Tommy's in a small stroller I've never seen before
and its wheels are buried in the snow but at least
he's got his snowsuit on. Laila's holding Miles's hand
and his other hand is wearing a glove so big the fingers are waving friendly in the wind. Which is weird
because Miles's eyes are always black marbles.

"Where's Mom?" I ask. My stomach's flipping
around worse than before our times tests in third
grade. No matter how hard I tried, I never passed
my nines.

"She's fine." Laila bends down to me. "She had to take your granny to the hospital, Britty-Bug. I think she's really sick. I'm sorry." I breathe out and realize I was holding my breath. Then I feel bad for being relieved Granny's sick and not Mom. We start walking.

"Are we going to see her?"

Laila tosses a curl out of her face with her bare hand, freckled and white in the cold. The stroller makes a painful squeak through the snow and I can tell Laila's pushing it as hard as she can. "Your mom said we should just wait at home. She'll call me when she knows more. You like pigs in a blanket?"

"Huh?"

"Little hot dogs in crescent rolls. It's Miles's favorite. Right, boo-boo?" Miles stares straight ahead and walks with his hands in fists. I look back and see the big glove dropped in the snow but don't say anything because turning the stroller around to go back for it would be ridiculous and I know Miles doesn't want that glove. "They're really good," Laila says. "You'll see."

• • •

Mom doesn't come home that night or the next or the next and the days are a gray blur like rain that drizzles just enough to keep you wet and cold. School is a long, exhausting dream even though Laila never gets me there until almost lunch. She works nights and the first night she leaves us with Tamara, who never looks up from her phone and puts Miles and Tommy to bed in their clothes. The next night it's Shonda and she makes Miles and Tommy a soapy bath and gives me two rows from her Hershey bar. She sings songs when she puts us to bed and keeps the TV low while she studies out of a huge book called *Fundamentals of Nursing*.

The next night it's supposed to be Jack but he never comes. I put Tommy to bed and leave Miles sitting on Granny's bed with his arms crossed and his shoes on because I don't know what else to do with him. Then I make my face as mean as it can be and sit on the couch staring at the front door, waiting for someone to rob us or kill us. A teeny part of me wants something bad to happen so Mom will get mad enough to leave Jack. But I ignore that part because I really am scared and don't want to be robbed or killed.

• • •

I wake up lying on the couch even though I don't remember falling asleep. When I get to school my class is at lunch but I'm not hungry because Laila gave me a peanut butter and butter sandwich on the way here. She called Jack every swear word I know plus some I didn't and stomped her boots in the slush like she was stomping on him and the sound of those words and the squish of the slush made me want to puke. Or maybe it was the sandwich.

Mr. McInnis drops his pen when I walk in the room the way I did when Ms. Sanogo told us about the rabbit in the moon. I haven't brushed my hair and I'm sure my eyes have dark rings like Mom's but I didn't look in the mirror. I have to look down to even remember what I'm wearing. "Hi," I say.

"Hey."

"Can I just sit at my desk? I'm not hungry. I'll be quiet."

Mr. McInnis nods. I don't think this is what he imagined for my future when he told me it was crazy bright and usually I'd be embarrassed but I'm just so tired. I let my backpack crash on the floor and rest my head on my arms on my desk and the world starts tipping but then Mr. McInnis touches my shoulder and I jerk back awake.

"Brittany?" He's sitting in Kenya's desk which is perfectly smooth and clean just like her skin and hair and shirts and everything. I want to cry thinking about how messy I am next to her. "How can I help?" Mr. McInnis asks.

I shrug. "My granny's sick," I say to the whiteboard. The numbers on it keep slipping down and I have to blink to keep them in line. "And she's not gonna get better." It's the first time I've said it out loud even though I've known since Shonda said the name of Granny's disease is Alzheimer's and when I asked how you fix it she just pushed her lips together and her eyes were "Silent Night" and she told me to *get some rest.* "And I'm so tired."

"I was close to my granny too," Mr. McInnis says.

"Did she die?"

"Yes."

"From Alzheimer's?"

"No." Mr. McInnis shakes his head like the memory of it sat on him like a fly. "I can't tell you anything that won't make it sad, but I can tell you that your memories of her will make you stronger. Even if you can't feel it happening. They're there, in your blood."

This makes no sense but just listening to Mr. McInnis's voice is nice. I look at the clock and there are twelve minutes left of lunch. "Do you mind if I just rest until math?" I ask and Mr. McInnis nods. He pats my shoulder again and goes back to his desk. I fall asleep like a dive into a deep, deep pool and dream of tiny Grannys floating on their backs in my veins, single file, in old-fashioned swimsuits and caps.

• • •

Mom's sitting next to an empty white hospital bed and I'm relieved there's no blood on it even though I don't think you get bloody when you die from

Alzheimer's. I'm also relieved Granny's body isn't in it because I know I would puke if I saw a dead body. Even if it was Granny's. Especially if it was Granny's. A few flurries are floating outside the window and the room is gray from the snow light. But the lamp next to the bed is on and it makes an orange circle on the white sheet. Mom is staring at it.

"I'm so sorry," Laila says. She rushes into the room like wind around a corner and hugs Mom's neck and Tommy whines and reaches for Mom and she takes him. He says "doo ba doo" to her and smacks his palm on her face and Mom smiles. "Sorry I had to bring them here," Laila says. "I just can't be late to work again or that maniac will fire me and I really need this job. I'm so sorry, Reen. I love you."

Mom stands up and hugs Laila again and tells her not to worry and thanks her for all her help during the blurry days. Then Laila leaves and takes all the air with her. All of a sudden it's so hot. "We just have to wait for the papers," Mom says. "Then we can go." She hugs me and it feels really good even though she's so skinny. "I missed you so much," she says. "I'm sorry I haven't been home. I just didn't know when Granny would . . . go . . . and I didn't want her to be alone."

I don't know what to say so I just say, "I'm sorry, Mom," like Laila did.

"I'm sorry for you, Brit. I know you loved Granny and she really loved you. You were so sweet to her. It made me so proud." I can hear the crying in her voice and I wish it would stop. If she cries, the whole world might melt into one big blue and green puddle, and Tommy and I will have to swim for our lives and how will I carry him and swim at the same time? I only ever had one swimming lesson. I shake my head because I'm thinking craziness again. Maybe it's the heat.

• • •

We leave the hospital at dinnertime and the bus is crowded with people going home from work. I hold Tommy in my lap and let him chew on my hair. Mom stands next to us swaying and catching herself, holding on to a strap. The snow's coming down hard and the bus moves slow. Some cars already crashed into each other and going around them makes the ride even slower. Police lights flash through the bus and all the faces turn red and blue, the way Mr. McInnis told us the blood goes to and from our hearts.

When we finally get home the house is black and I rush to turn on the lamp for Granny and at the very same second the light clicks on, I realize she is dead. The couch is empty and I can see the scratch marks from Patches that Granny's legs usually covered up. I run to my room and fall onto my bed and cry and cry, about a whole lot of things. Granny and Patches and never getting away from Jack and Mom not eating. And Granny again.

The microwave's humming in the kitchen and Mom's pouring out dry rice. Tommy is banging his hands on his tray, waiting. But Granny isn't sitting at the table. How will I ever do homework without Granny next to me? I cry more than I've ever cried. I wonder if my body will run out of tears and I'll have to drink water to make more. I remember the time Granny told me to put a barrette in my hair and (maybe) called me pretty. No one will ever notice my tangled hair again.

Mom sits down next to me and puts her hand on my back. She's not crying and I'm thankful for that. "Do you think you could eat something?" she asks. "I made red beans and rice." I shake my head into my pillow and think of how Granny pulled all the sausage out of her red beans and rice and fed it to Patches. Will everything always remind me of Granny forever? "Okay," Mom says. "Just tell me if you change your mind." She kisses the back of my head and I feel the whisper of her leaving. The way Granny left.

Much, much later I stop crying. I pull the Plan B notebook out from under the mattress and go into the kitchen. Mom's at the table, just sitting. "Hungry?" she asks but I shake my head. I lay the notebook down in front of her. It looks very small.

"I tried to make a Plan B but I couldn't," I say. I want to tell her that it's not my job because I'm only eleven and she's supposed to make the plan.

But I'm too sad and too tired and so is she. I can tell because the dirty dishes are stacked up like a junk pile in the sink. "You should call Uncle Fuzzy and tell him about Granny," I tell her. "He'll want to know. His number is on page thirteen." Then I go to bed and sleep so deep I have no dreams at all.

• • •

I thought it would feel good to be back at school like after Thanksgiving but my body's so heavy and my head can't wake up. Mr. McInnis tells me not to worry about my homework until I feel better and talks to me the way we talked to Patches when we found him. Marisol hugs me in the hall and tells me something about Leon but I can't focus on her words. It's so loud and everything's buzzing. After lunch, Mr. McInnis sends me to the nurse.

• • •

I'm sitting on the couch in Granny's spot with my eyes closed thinking about what she looked like so I won't forget. But her face is already soft in my mind like a picture out of focus. It feels like someone switched my brain with a cotton ball. Mom calls me to dinner and I don't want to go because I don't want to leave Granny's spot and I don't want to feel her empty chair next to me. But I get up because it's important to Mom that we eat as a *family.* That word sounds different now. Like when you can't remember how to spell a word you've known since kindergarten.

Dinner's a blur like everything until Jack gets a text that the electric bill is five days late.

"I just forgot to pay it," Mom says. "I'll do it tomorrow."

I wait for Jack to say, *If we have any lights tomorrow. You have to pay the bills, Maureen. What do you do all day, anyway?*

But he doesn't say any of it because Mom's looking straight at him and her eyes are arrow tips. Then everything gets buzzy again.

thirteen

Marisol and me are the only ones who wanted a spot on the monkey bars because the wind's blowing little bits of ice. The rest of the girls are huddled against the brick wall complaining about being outside and the boys are kicking a half-pumped soccer ball through a tan patch of grass. I can hear Marisol talking again. She's telling me about the notes she trades with Leon in the hall and we're thinking about what they mean.

"I think he likes you," I say.

"You do?"

163

"Yeah."

"Oooh, girl. I hope you're right. Whenever I see him my whole body tingles all over like shivering but not cold."

I smile. We sit quiet for a minute.

"I'm really sorry about your granny," Marisol says.

"Thanks. I miss her."

"I know you do." Marisol puts her arm around my shoulders and we don't talk about Leon or Granny or anything. We just sit with the ice smacking our faces and it feels like we're the only two people in the world. With Marisol as my friend, I could probably be an Eskimo.

. . .

I'm lying on my bed searching my social studies packet for one more fact about Saul Alinsky when Mom shows up in my doorway holding my Plan B notebook. "I read your plan," she says. "It's really good."

I roll my eyes even though she hates that. "Except

that it's not a plan. It's just a bunch of nothing." I look back down. I can't remember the motto of the Back of the Yards Neighborhood Council.

"Don't say that. There's so much good stuff in here. Can I keep it for a while? I promise to take good care of it."

"Yeah. Sure. I don't need it." Then I find it: *We the people will work out our own destiny.*

"I got you something," Mom says and hands me a new roll of blue tape to hang up the rest of my art that's been piling up in a corner of my room since Thanksgiving.

"Thanks."

I wait for her to go make dinner or fold laundry but instead she sits down on my bed and just watches me roll each piece of tape into a circle and push all the projects onto the wall, even the happy hot dog. Jerome's family crest was the best. He sketched a huge hawk for Hawkins with its wings out wide flying through a dark gray sky. He did it with a regular number two pencil. Mr. McInnis called it *purposeful*. I hope Jerome still has that hawk. Maybe it's on a wall somewhere in Baltimore. But probably boys don't do that.

When I finish, my whole wall's covered with art even though we haven't even gotten to winter break. "It looks amazing," Mom says.

"Yeah." Then Tommy wakes up from his nap and Mom goes to get him and I lie back on my bed and think about how good it feels to sit in Mr. McInnis's class and paint or draw the things from our lives even if some of them turn out weird.

Mom pokes her head back in. "Brittany." I look up and back at her so she's upside down. "Don't give up on me."

• • •

Even though we never got the hang of multiplying fractions, Mr. McInnis moved us on to decimals. I guess if we're gonna get through the whole math book by June we just have to keep going. We told him no teacher ever gets through the whole math book by June but Mr. McInnis just looked at us like he can't believe we're still comparing him to any other teacher.

I can't get my decimal point in the right place. My whole sheet's filled with little red arrows pointing left or right. If you put them all together, my point would probably end up right back where it started. Like when they pose us for our class picture and we move a little to the left then a little to the right until the teacher taking the picture says *Perfect!* but we're all standing exactly where we stood in the first place. Just like our whole lives.

• • •

I'm trying not to smile too much so Tonio doesn't think I'm weird but it's hard because I'm riding next to my best friend in a car that doesn't belong to a grown-up and for the first time in my whole life I feel a little free. Marisol's scrolling through her iPad with her earbuds in because she's used to being free but I'm trying to memorize everything. Like the way Tonio turns through the crackly radio to find the Spanish station and how he sings quiet so

Marisol can sing loud. I can't believe Mom let me go but I guess since she read my Plan B notebook and knows I took the 82 and 56 buses by myself this is nothing.

Out the window everyone's shoveling sidewalks or waiting for the bus or carrying grocery bags or walking dogs or talking to themselves or smoking cigarettes so Chicago looks like it always does, but today all the colors look brighter even though it's winter. I want to hug everyone. Even Cart Man, who would definitely push me away.

"We're here!" Marisol snaps her seat belt off and pushes the car door open.

"Whoa, let me park first." Tonio's laughing and looking at us in the rearview mirror.

"Thanks for the ride," I tell him.

"Anytime."

Marisol and I climb up the snowbank and down the other side to the ice. It's the first time they ever had ice in this park because when it got really cold an old man who lives across the street decided to turn on his hose and flood it. I saw him on the news. "These kids need something to do," he said and went back into his house and the reporter said, "Well. There you have it."

The ice is packed and most people have on boots but Marisol has brand-new skates and I have her old ones. We sit down on a bench to put them on. "Lace 'em tight," she tells me.

"How come you know about skating?"

"My papi used to take me."

"Oh."

"Since he died Mamá tries to keep life the same." She's pulling on each row of laces, working her way to the top. "So every year I try on my skates and if I need new ones she buys them. But she never takes me skating. So it's not really the same." She double-knots the bow and says, "Race ya!" and stomps through the snow until she gets to the ice and rolls smooth like a marble into the center of the crowd.

I finish lacing my skates and walk to the edge. I haven't skated since Mom took me in second grade. She had a good tip day and usually that meant she stuffed the extra money into a mason jar under her bed but instead we took the L downtown and skated late into the night until there were hardly any people left and then we found a coffee shop and ordered the biggest hot chocolates they had. I made a beard with the whipped cream and pretended I was Santa Claus and Mom laughed so hard.

"C'mon!" Marisol says. Her face is huge and bright in front of mine, like the moon looks over the parking lot sometimes.

I dig the toe of one skate into the snow. "I'm not a good skater."

"We'll go slow." Marisol takes my hand and I step out and I'm wobbly but we keep going until I get smoother and she lets go.

• • •

"Ho, ho, ho!" Laila calls from behind a huge Christmas tree in our doorway.

"Are you crazy?" Mom says through the branches.

"Prob'ly! Help me get it inside!" So they pull the tree in and needles go everywhere but Mom doesn't care, which is not like her. But nobody's like themselves around Laila. "Is it not the most beautiful tree you've ever seen?" Laila asks but we all know the answer. It's like the tree got lost and came to the wrong house. It takes up half the room.

"Where'd you get it?" Mom asks. She's looking at the top branch brushing the ceiling.

"I stole it."

Mom gives Laila drop-dead eyes and she laughs. "I'm kidding! You think I'd actually steal a Christmas tree? Don't answer that. I won it. We had a drawing at work and I snuck my name in five times." She holds one finger up to her mouth like *shhhh* and I laugh.

"Don't you want to keep it?" Mom asks.

"I already got one."

"You? Got a tree?"

"No, Dominic got it for me. Decorated it and everything."

"Who's Dominic?"

"Girl! I will *tell you later,* if you know what I mean." Mom shakes her head and I wonder if Marisol will ever say to me, *Girl! I will tell you later!* I hope so. "You got a tree stand?" Laila asks and Mom

shrugs with her hands like *What do you think?* "No worries. I'll get you one." She leans the tree in the corner. "You got a beer?"

"That I have," Mom says and they go into the kitchen.

I sit in Granny's spot and stare at the tree and suck the pine smell as deep as I can into my lungs. Tommy's hitting the lowest branch and laughing when it bounces and I wish Granny was here because that's the kind of thing she liked before her mind got muddy. Babies doing simple things.

I'm not trying to listen to Laila and Mom but Laila's voice is so loud. She says something about Jack with a girl besides Mom and my heart cracks like a frozen puddle, with one piece furious and one embarrassed and one confused and on and on. But the biggest piece is relief because maybe now we'll get out of here.

I go into the kitchen pretending to get some water to see Mom's reaction but her heart cracked into one giant piece: terrified.

fourteen

Ms. Sanogo's class is watching movies because she says getting kids to work the day before winter break is like asking butterflies to line up in row. But our class is celebrating Yule. Yesterday Mr. McInnis brought in pine branches to make Yule wreaths but the assistant principal said they'd look too much like Christmas wreaths so we're making bird feeders instead. Mr. McInnis says seeds and feeding creatures are an important part of Yule. The boys liked it for a while because of the hammers but now they're mostly pelting each other with birdseed when Mr.

McInnis isn't looking and sometimes when he is.

I don't flutter in my chair like a butterfly or throw birdseed or pass notes or anything because I'm not celebrating. I'm thinking about two whole weeks at home and Mom's terrified eyes and our empty cabinet and how cold it was on Thanksgiving.

Laila never got us a tree stand so Mom put the trunk in a bucket she got me a million years ago when I was a regular kid who went to the beach and dug in the sand with a purple plastic shovel. We couldn't find our box of Christmas lights and I tried to get Mom to at least get the twenty-four Christmas balls at Walgreens for $5.99 but she couldn't and I knew it but I was hungry and frustrated and said in a spitting voice, "Who has a naked Christmas tree leaning in the corner in a beach bucket? That's so ghetto." I waited for Mom to be mad but she just told me not to use that word.

"Brittany." I jump and knock over my birdfeeder and the seeds go everywhere. Kenya starts picking them up and seeing her clean, ironed khaki knees on the floor makes me sick to my stomach. I drop

down next to her. "You don't have to pick them up," I say, trying to get them faster than her. "I spilled them."

"Yeah, but I startled you." We put all the seeds back in the feeder and Kenya sets it gently on my desk. "I just wanted to tell you there's a nail sticking out," she says, pointing to one corner. "I didn't want you to get hurt."

"Thanks," I whisper because tears are stinging my eyes and Kenya sees them but she just smiles politely and slides back into her desk.

• • •

Mom's not waiting for me after school so I just start walking. Everyone's running more than usual because their backpacks are light as feathers but mine's full of books. You can only check out two at a time but the librarian let me take twelve. I guess she felt sorry for me because I couldn't stop crying after Kenya helped me and Mr. McInnis sent me to the library instead of the office because we only have a social worker on Tuesdays.

At the end of the block the blue and gray bird

with the Mohawk is sitting in his empty tree with his mean eyes and he looks right at me and squawks. "Here," I tell him and hang the bird feeder on the bottom branch. "Happy Yule." He tips his head at me and bobs a little. "Now stop being such a jerk."

· · ·

One time a lady came to school to teach us *stress management* and every time Jack goes crazy I breathe just like she said. Slow and deep and from my stomach. But no matter how I breathe my brain keeps making plans. *If he really hurts her this time, where should I look for Mom's phone first? What if it's not charged? Should I run next door? Do I take Tommy? What if he's asleep?* When Granny was still here, Mom told me sometimes she'd lie in bed at night trying to figure out how to save me and Tommy and Granny if the house caught on fire. This is kind of like that.

Then the yelling stops and I sneak down the hall to the bathroom like I have to pee. I can hear better from here but there's nothing so I wait, sitting on the closed toilet staring at the shower curtain which almost touches my knees because the bathroom's very small. It's covered with lilacs and I try to count the petals on one but the rows aren't even and I keep getting lost. Then I hear Mom's voice and let my breath out so I guess I wasn't managing stress after all.

"He's your son," she says. She's right next to the wall so I stand up and lean my face against it like trying to reach her. Jack says something I can't hear. "You know he is," Mom says quietly. "I'm not talking about me, or Brittany. Jack, I can't buy diapers. I can't even feed him. Please." Even though I can't see her I know she's looking down. But it doesn't work. I hear the bedroom door slam and then the front door too. I wait a long time to see if Mom will cry but she doesn't. Or if she does, she hides it in her pillow.

• • •

Odessa and Tiny are on the porch hanging Christmas lights. Odessa's got a Santa hat on with a bell that jingles just like her wind chimes. I put on my coat and stand at the fence where she told me about

God laughing when people make plans. "Can I help?" I ask in my small mouse voice.

Tiny looks up and says nothing but Odessa says, "Sure, baby! Come on over." I run over quick but walk up the steps slow. "I could use some young fingers help me straighten this mess out." Odessa hands me a tangle of lights. "My arthritis real bad tonight." I pull the strands through and around each other and Odessa passes them to Tiny who's so tall he tapes them right onto the ceiling with no ladder.

We keep going like that, me untangling and Odessa handing them up and Tiny taping. No one says a word, which is not like Odessa, but it's one of those moments that's better off quiet. There are a million lights and the porch gets brighter and softer and pretty soon it's shining gold. We have one strand left and Odessa goes in to get an extension cord.

"Brittany." Mom's at the top of our steps holding her sweater wrapped tight with her arms crossed. It's weird to see her from here, like I'm in space looking down. She looks small and helpless like

Patches and I wish it was as easy as giving Mom some milk and a new name.

"Hi, Mom. We're almost done. Odessa just went in to get a cord." Mom nods at me and then at Tiny. He nods back. "Doesn't it look beautiful?"

"It does."

"Come over!"

"No, I gotta—"

"Mom! Come over! Just for a sec." And she does! She runs over in her socks just like me and her breath puffs out little clouds and Odessa comes back out and we finish the last one and all of us just stand there in the gold light.

Tiny says, "Hope heaven feel like this."

And Odessa laughs rumbly and says, "For you it will, baby. For you it will."

• • •

I didn't even realize what day it was until I asked Mom why we were eating dinner (if you call one can of tuna and lots of mayonnaise dinner) at four o'clock and she said, "It's Christmas Eve. And we're going to church." On my bed was a dress and tights and shoes and even a black velvet headband laid out in the shape of a person and I thought, *I wish I could really be that person.* "Where'd you get the money?" I asked.

But Mom said, "Don't worry about it." She put Tommy in a little green suit that was too tight but since he's a baby he looked adorable anyway and we got on the bus like some kind of regular family.

We get off at the corner and walk down the block and the church is enormous, not like the little red brick church we used to go to at the old apartment when it was just Mom and me and she was tired but never terrified. A little black and white sign on the church says *Our Lady of Sorrows* and I look up at Mom and know exactly what that means. "Maybe we should go somewhere else," I say but Mom says, "No, let's go in. It's supposed to be beautiful inside."

It is. The walls are pink and blue like baby blankets and the lamps shine like silk and there are arches and statues everywhere. I hold Mom's hand because I get dizzy from being so small. Tommy fussed the whole way here but even he's quiet now. Some of the people smile at us and we smile back, still pretending to be a regular family. Mom's better at it than anyone. She walks straight up like *nothing to hide* and picks a pew in the middle and we slide in.

Then I look up and the whole ceiling is covered in daisies. "Granny!" I whisper and Mom looks up too. There must be a million of them, daisy sculptures, all beaming down at us and I'm sure they've been here forever but it still feels like a sign from heaven and I don't even believe in heaven. I spend the whole Mass like that (except when I have to look down to pray), staring at those white daisies in their blue boxes of sky, feeling Granny smiling down on me, which is the best Christmas present I could ever get.

• • •

Someone's knocking on the door. It's not that late but it's late enough. A tiny part of me hopes it's Jack with the money Mom needs but most of me hopes it's not. Anyway he wouldn't knock. Mom's frozen on the couch like Granny used to be and the knocking starts again. "Should I see who it is?" I ask but Mom doesn't answer or even move her head.

"Brittany?" a girl's voice says and I run to the window and peek through the blinds and it's Agata!

I turn all the locks quick and swing the door open and Agata smiles. Her hair's still long and perfect and blond and her glasses are still black and smart but this time she's got on lipstick and a church coat and high heels. *"Wesołych Świąt!"* she says and I blink and she laughs. "That's 'Merry Christmas.'"

"Merry Christmas!" I tell her and hug her tight and she laughs again. "Good to see you too." Then she yells something in Polish to the car on the street and a boy her age ducks his head down so he can see us. He gives her a thumbs-up and waves to me. He might be her brother or cousin or boyfriend but either way my heart leaps that Agata's with someone so nice.

"Aren't you going to invite her in?" Mom says.

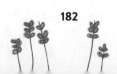

"Uh, yeah." Agata steps in and I wish the couch wasn't scratched up and covered in laundry but at least it's folded and Mom and I are still in our church dresses and our hair's brushed. "Mom, this is . . ."

"Agata," Mom says because she read my Plan B notebook so now she knows everything. Almost. "I'm Maureen."

They shake hands and Agata says, "So nice to meet you."

"Thanks for being so kind to Brittany at U Stasi," Mom says. "It means a lot."

"Of course. She's a great kid." I blush, partly because Agata thinks I'm great and partly because she thinks I'm a kid.

Agata opens her purse and pulls out a Christmas card and for a heartbeat I think *She found my dad* and he sent a card to say he's sorry for abandoning us for twelve years but now he's rich from some mathematical equation he invented and we can all live together in the Polish countryside. But when Agata opens it there's just a huge church wafer inside with Mary and Baby Jesus carved on it. "I brought *opłatek*," she says.

And Mom says, "Oh!" the way she did when I hit her with a squirt gun last summer. I was aiming for Jack but chickened out at the last second.

"It's a Polish Christmas Eve tradition," Agata tells me. She breaks the wafer and hands me half. "For you, Brittany, I wish love and peace and happiness for the year to come."

"Thank you," I whisper because I can't believe Agata's here at all and now she's making a wish for me.

"Now you break off a piece and eat it," Agata says. I do, and even though it looks pretty it tastes just like the wafers at Our Lady of Sorrows.

"Now you do the same for Agata," Mom says and I stare at her because she knows more about my dad than she says. I make a wish for Agata and she hugs me again and goes back to the car with the nice boy driving and Mom and I just look at each other.

Mom breaks off a piece of her wafer and holds

it out to me. "I wish you more love than you can imagine," she says. Her wafer tries to stick on my tongue but I force it down.

I break off a piece for Mom. There's so many wishes she needs I don't know where to start so I just say, "You too."

• • •

The days between Christmas and back to school are so boring I can't even count them down because every time I try it's still the same day. We haven't seen Jack since before Christmas Eve and Mom took us to the food bank which gave us two huge boxes because we were *first-time users* so we're not hungry now but what happens the second time? Plus Tommy's sick so Mom's spending most of her time worrying and taking his temperature which is why I was so surprised when she said, "Do you want to have a friend over today?"

Marisol on our doorstep is like a double rainbow, like catching the ice cream truck, like daisies on the ceiling. When I open the door we shriek and hug and jump up and down so I guess she was bored too. It's strange how two days back to back can be so different. Marisol starts talking before I even get the door locked and she has a whole bag full of magazines and a whole iPad full of songs. We're chirping like birds at each other and I can hear how dumb it sounds but I don't care. We go into my room and I look back at Mom and her eyes are ancient memories.

fifteen

Mr. McInnis writes *New Year's resolution* **on the** whiteboard in two different colors and stands in front of it, grinning at us. Something about him looks new even though his hair and glasses and clothes are the same. "I learned a new verse for 'This Land Is Your Land' over the break," he says. But that can't be it. One song verse couldn't make someone that happy. But then I think of Marisol so maybe it can. We sing the regular verses, then we add:

"There was a big high wall there that tried to
  stop me
Sign was painted said 'Private Property'
But on the backside, it didn't say nothing
This land was made for you and me."

"My New Year's resolution is to follow my heart,"
Mr. McInnis says. "And not to worry too much
about the rules." This sounds pretty dangerous to
me and I hope he doesn't get fired for following his
heart because this school's all about rules and we all
need Mr. McInnis.

It takes me a long time to think of my resolution and by the time I scribble it down most of the
class is taking out their science books. I write, *Treat
every day like a beginning.* Because today really
does feel like the beginning of something. It could
be the new year or Mr. McInnis's new verse or the
fact that I walked to school by myself (just because
Tommy's still sick and Mom didn't want to take him
in the cold, but still) but it also feels like the beginning of something else I can't explain.

• • •

We're back at the hospital where Granny died. Where we left her body and took the paper with the number on it that told us to wait six to eight weeks to know where they buried her. "Mom," I'd whispered. "Granny's not an Indian."

And Mom said, "Not Indian. Indigent." I didn't ask her what it meant but the next time we went to computer lab I got on the dictionary site and asked Mr. McInnis how to spell it and he blushed so I thought it was a bad word, but the dictionary just said *lacking money, very poor.* And Granny was that.

I feel terrible that Mom has to be back here where they used a show-off word to call Granny poor. That she has to sit in this waiting room where maybe she sat with Granny, with all these people bent over or barely dressed or moaning or all three. Did Granny sit here too? Did she see all this or were her eyes already clouds?

The lady behind the glass calls Mom's name even though she just turned in pages and pages of papers about Tommy. She holds up a clipboard. "I forgot a page!" she calls but Tommy starts the gravel cough and Mom doesn't move.

"I'll get it," I say and bring back the clipboard with its pen swinging off the side, attached with green yarn. Tommy's still coughing and Mom's holding him close with her head against the wall and her eyes closed. The Scrabble box is in her lap. "Can you fill it out for me, Brit? Is it complicated? You can just read me the questions."

I look at the sheet. It's only four questions and it doesn't look hard. It doesn't even look like a real hospital form. "I can do it," I tell her.

1. Is your partner emotionally abusive? Does s/he ever call you names, act possessive or jealous, or accuse you of things you didn't do?

I circle YES.

2. Is your partner physically abusive? Does s/he ever kick, grab, push, punch, or choke you?

190

I circle YES.

3. Are you afraid of your partner?

I circle YES.

4. Would you like to speak to a victim advocate today about your safety and options?

This one's harder. I look at Mom. Her eyes are still closed and I don't know what a victim advocate is but I know Mom doesn't want to speak to one. But I want to hear about safety and I want to hear about options.

I circle YES.

• • •

We wait a long time with all the undressed, upset people. The sun climbs down the sky and hits the office buildings and turns the windows orange and I remember how this morning I thought something was beginning and feel stupid.

They call Mom's name and we go into a room

where there's a girl Agata's age. She has wavy hair the color of sand and wears all black except for a hot pink hat, nail polish, and lipstick. I'm not sure why she still has her hat on because it's really warm in the room.

"Hi," she says. "Have a seat."

Mom blinks at her, confused about why she's not a nurse. Tommy's almost asleep in Mom's arms and I know he's heavy but Mom doesn't sit. "Did you . . . need something?" she asks.

"My name's Haley," the girl says. "I'm a victim advocate here at the hospital and I see you wanted to talk about your safety and hear about some options today."

Mom stares at her.

Haley holds up the form I filled out. "Sorry. This is yours, right?"

Mom squints at it and sighs. "Brittany." I look at her but don't say anything because there's nothing to say. "I'm sorry," Mom tells Haley. "This is a misunderstanding. My daughter filled out that form and I think she was confused about the questions. We're fine. Everything's fine."

Haley looks at me and I'm embarrassed about my faded clothes and tangled hair but I stare back at her hoping she'll push Mom harder, the way Mr. McInnis tells Ms. Sanogo we need to be pushed.

"Oh, okay," Haley says. "Well, here's my card." She hands Mom a little white card with a pink flower on it, the same color as her lipstick and hat and nails. Is it part of her uniform, the way everyone at Walmart wears blue shirts? "We have all kinds of services," Haley says. "Court advocacy, shelter, counseling. We have a twenty-four-hour crisis line that you can call anytime with any questions or if you need resources. We have children's groups and support groups. So please don't hesitate. Even if you just want to talk."

Mom smiles with half her mouth. "Thanks," she says and takes the card. Tommy coughs and turns his head on Mom's chest. We move toward the waiting room but Mom turns back to Haley. For half a second, my heart jumps like someone shocked it with one of those machines hanging on the wall. "Does that form . . . go anywhere?" Mom asks and Haley shakes her head like she knows what Mom means even though I don't.

"No," Haley says. "It's completely confidential." Mom nods and Tommy coughs and we walk through the door with Haley calling after us, "I hope he feels better!" We sit down in the waiting room in the same chairs to wait some more. The sky turns dark blue and I'm starving, but nothing else is different.

• • •

I'm missing school but Mom has no way to get me there because she won't let me ride the bus alone even though I already rode the 82 and 56 by myself (twice). I sit by the window in Tommy's hospital room and watch the wind blow the top layer of snow off the banks and around and around because there's nothing else to do. I wonder if Mr. McInnis is worried about me the way he was about Jerome. I wonder if he called Mom's phone and if she'd tell me if he did.

This is our third morning here, I think. All the days and nights feel the same. The hall lights are always blinding and the beeps are always loud. The nurses always come to check Tommy's vitals. Even if Mom just spent an hour patting him to sleep. They just wake him back up. One of them says "So sorry, little prince" and that's nice of her. I've never, ever been this bored but I don't say anything because Tommy's never been this sick and Mom's never been this worried.

But this morning's a little different because the doctor's supposed to tell us if the IV can come out and Tommy can eat cereal and drink his bottle. (He barely cried when they stuck the needle in his foot. He's braver than me.) This seems like good news but I can't tell because Mom doesn't seem less worried.

The door opens but it's not the doctor. It's Jack, who hasn't been to the hospital one time. His eyes are zigzags and he keeps sniffing like he has a cold. He shouldn't be here with germs around Tommy because the nurses say his immune system is sensitive. Maybe a nurse will notice and kick him out but probably not. Mom is sitting on a chair next to Tommy's bed and doesn't stand up or move or say anything.

"Hey," Jack says. He stands in the space between the door and the room that's full of shadows and looks over at Tommy like he's afraid to come closer. "How's he doin'?"

"Better," Mom says.

"Oh, thank God. Sorry I ain't been around before. I just been . . . you know."

Mom stares at him.

"Hospitals, you know," Jack says. "I just . . . you know. Anyway." If Jack wrote a paper for Mr. McInnis, it would come back covered in red ink. This thought makes me crazy happy and I smile. Jack sees me but looks away. "So, I'm so glad he's better. I gotta run 'cause I gotta meet this guy, he's gonna, we got this thing and I'll see you back at home, okay?" He backs out of the room the way Mom does when she's done vacuuming and says *My mother taught me that.* The door clicks shut.

I look at Mom and raise my eyebrows and she laughs, but by accident. Like when you're drinking something and it goes down wrong and you start coughing and coughing. That's how her laugh is. She keeps laughing and laughing like she doesn't mean to but can't stop. The doctor comes in and I wait for his cold stare like we shouldn't be laughing when Tommy's so sick but he doesn't give us one. Instead he smiles wide and his eyes are big behind the thick rims of his glasses and he says, "That's the best sound I've heard today."

"Me too," I say.

• • •

It's the middle of the afternoon and Tommy's restless because he feels better after his milk and cereal and he's tired of watching *Sesame Street* and all the other shows on channel 2 and so am I. It's so many hours till dinner I don't bother to count. I want to take a walk in the hallway but I don't think Tommy's supposed to leave the room and Mom won't let me go by myself. The doctor said Tommy can go home tomorrow if he keeps eating and drinking. His cheeks are a little pink but his belly's so scrawny.

I sit him next to me in the middle of the hospital bed and push the button so the bed goes as high as it can. He crawls around in a little circle then sits back down, like Patches used to on the couch. We get so high I reach up to see if I can touch the ceiling but I can't. "That's enough, Brit," Mom's voice says from under us. "Come back down." I push the other button and we come down slow and Tommy bounces up and down like he does when his toys play music. When we hit the bottom Mom is next to us, holding my Plan B notebook. She hands it to me and when I hold it again I realize how much I've missed it, even if my Plan B was for nothing. Maybe someday when I'm older and have self-determination I'll make a Plan C.

"Thanks," I tell Mom. "Why are you giving it back?"

"Just ready to. I called Uncle Fuzzy and asked him your last question, about Lily," she says and sits back down in the hospital chair that's so familiar now it seems like we're in our living room. "He said

Granny's dad named her and all her sisters after Alabama wildflowers. Violet was the oldest, then Laurel, then Uncle Fuzzy, then Daisy, and Lily was the youngest. So Lily was Granny's little sister." I stare at Mom. I hear her words but it seems like she's reading from a script. "She was only a year younger than Granny and Fuzzy said Granny loved her more than anything."

I start to cry which is surprising because I thought my tears were used up. I think it's because I loved Granny more than anything and I never got to tell her. Tommy looks at me like I'm a toy making a new sound and pulls my hair. I might also be crying because I'm so relieved Tommy didn't die like Granny. Then Mom does a crazy, crazy, crazy thing. She takes Haley's card out of her purse (I can see the hot pink flower) and picks up her phone.

Sixteen

We're as close to the Willis Tower as we've ever been.
We're almost to the lake, which is covered in gray
ice because the winter's the coldest it's ever been.
I saw it on the news at the hospital. The lake's the
same color as the sky and the smoke from the buildings and the buildings themselves. It makes Chicago
look like the saddest place on earth, which should
make it easy to leave but doesn't because all I can
think about is if Odessa can come out of her house
with the arthritis and how I can't bring her hot soup

like she got Mom Gatorade. And mostly how I'll never see her again. Or Mr. McInnis. Or Marisol.

The bus lurches to a stop like throwing up and Mom's already in the aisle, holding Tommy over her shoulder and the Scrabble box in her other hand. I've spent so much time trying to get to Montgomery and I don't even know what it's like. Maybe it's worse than Chicago. Maybe Jack will find us there or we won't find Fuzzy or all the kids will think I'm weird. "Maybe we should just go home," I tell Mom.

She says, "Stand up."

I stand. The cold from the open bus door gusts down the aisle and sneaks under my coat. I start to shiver and I can't stop. Mom hands me the Scrabble box. "Can you carry this?" I nod and Mom bends down so her face is right in front of mine. Her eyes are the color of the lake in summer and I wonder if it's still that color underneath all the ice and if the fish are cold. "It's gonna be okay," she says. We get off the bus.

It's seven blocks to the Greyhound station and

we walk pressed together like we'll stay warmer that way. I can feel ice in my eyelashes. "Aren't you scared?" I ask.

"Of what?"

"Of Jack. Finding us."

"Jack's doing his own thing now," Mom says. "And we're doing ours."

I can't believe it's that simple but Mom's never been wrong about Jack. Like the time she wouldn't turn the heat up and he did come home and his voice bounced off the walls like a superball and she calmed him down with a bunch of beers popped in a row. I don't understand any of it but all I can do is walk on the gray sidewalk through the gray city and trust her.

• • •

Haley's waiting for us outside the station wearing her pink hat and matching pink mittens. When she sees us she tucks her phone in her coat pocket like we're the most important thing. "Hi, guys!" Her voice is chirpy like meeting best friends at the movies. I wonder what she'll do after this. Just go back to the hospital and have a regular day? "Let's go get the tickets," she says.

I follow Mom and Haley to the ticket window and every turned shoulder looks like Jack's. It's so crowded. I squeeze the Scrabble box tight. Haley counts out perfect twenties for the lady behind the glass and pushes the stack through and the lady pushes an envelope back. "Transfer in Nashville," she says. "Gate six."

Haley hands Mom the envelope and says, "I'll walk you." So we walk to Gate 6. It's not far, around a corner and down some stairs. Still no Jack. I'm holding the Scrabble box so tight my thumbs are white. The bus is already there, rumbling low and puffing smoke out the back. "Well, I guess this is goodbye," Haley says. "Good luck with everything! I know you'll do great." She hugs Mom and kisses me on top of the head, then pats Tommy's back gently so he doesn't wake up.

"Thanks," Mom says. "You are one in a million."

We climb the steps of the bus. There are only three people inside and none of them is Jack. We wait and wait. More people get on but not Jack. Finally the driver hops up the steps like onto a stage and stands facing us. He's thin with perfect dreads tied behind his neck with a plain white string and glasses with blue rims. "Hey, y'all," he says. "My name's Marcel and I'm your ride to Nashville. The Music City. Just sit back and enjoy. We're ready to go." He sits down and pulls the huge handle and the door sucks shut. The bus starts to move.

Haley waves with both arms and I force one of my hands to let go of the Scrabble box to wave back. We pull out from under the bridge into the world. Mom's smiling at all the buildings like wishing them goodbye but they're still as stones. In a minute we're on the expressway. Mom closes her eyes and lays her cheek on Tommy's head but I turn around in my seat to watch until the Willis Tower is out of sight.

• • •

Early in the morning, after we make the transfer in Nashville (the Music City) at two-thirty, which is like a strange dream, Mom and Tommy are still asleep and the sun's rising over the city of Birmingham. It has some tall buildings but nothing like Chicago which makes it feel friendlier even though I know some bad things happened here once because Mr. McInnis was just starting to teach us about civil rights before Tommy got pneumonia and we met Haley and got on a bus.

"But don't let Chicago fool you," Mr. McInnis told us, because Martin Luther King Jr. himself got hit with a rock in Chicago when he was marching for better houses. We had to memorize part of a speech Dr. King gave in Chicago in 1966 and most of the class had to read their lines but I still know mine by heart: *This is freedom. This is a weapon greater than any force you can name. Once you know this, and know it with all your being, you will move and act with a determination and power that the federal government cannot ignore, that the school boards cannot overlook, and that the housing authority cannot dismiss.* Mr. McInnis smiled at me when I finished. Probably he liked the school boards part.

The Scrabble box is on my lap. I look over at Mom but her hair's bouncing over her face with the highway bumps and her breaths are slow so I know she's deep asleep. I open the box. It's full of old pictures and cards and drawings I made in school. Our birth certificates are in there and Tommy's hospital bracelet from when he was born and his pink and blue striped baby hat and a little ziplock bag labeled BRITTANY'S TOOTH. I hold it up and sure enough there's a tiny tooth inside with a dot of blood on top.

Some of the pictures are old. Grandma Jane holding Mom when she was little in front of a Ferris wheel. Granny way before she died, sitting in a lawn chair and looking sideways and laughing. There are a few pictures of Tommy, propped up next to his Easter basket and in the swing at the purple slide playground and in his high chair with broccoli in his hair. But most of the pictures are of me.

• • •

Fuzzy's waiting at the bus station outside a beat-up blue pick-up truck. He has on jeans and a short-sleeve plaid shirt and a bow tie like he's meeting someone important but still being himself. Mom didn't tell me which one he was but I knew any-way. Just one of those things. He was wearing a baseball cap but as soon as the bus pulled up he took it off and curled up the brim so it would fit in his back pocket and smoothed what's left of his hair across the top of his head. A few gray wisps like they draw the wind in kids' books. Then he just looked up at the bus and grinned.

He's still smiling when we come down the steps, taking turns holding the driver's hand, into the bright sun bright sky of Montgomery. It's nine in the morning and it's weird to be starting a new day when we didn't really finish the old one. "Hey, Maureen!" Fuzzy calls and he hugs Mom and pats her back. "I'd know that pretty smile anywhere, just like your mama. Hey, little man." He makes a clicking noise at Tommy and holds out his hands but Tommy frowns at him and Fuzzy laughs deeper than I expected from a man so skinny and old. "Don't wanna come to no goofball, hey? I don't blame you."

Then Fuzzy bends down to me and his eyes are the same blue as Mom's but cloudy like different weather's coming. "And you must be Brittany."

I say, "Yes, sir," because Mom told me to say that in Alabama.

"I'm so glad y'all came. Are ya hungry?"

"Not too much," I say. "Sir."

Fuzzy finds the huge suitcase the nurse at the hospital gave us and somehow swings it up into the back of the truck like a superhero with invisible muscles. Then we all squish in, me right next to Fuzzy who smells like aftershave and something like cigarettes but not quite. "I'll swing ya through downtown," he says. "So you can see your new city."

Our new city's white and shimmery in the sunlight. Fuzzy drives with his window down and waves to everyone he sees and they all wave back. The air feels fuller and kinder than in Chicago and pink flowers are blooming on bushes all around the capitol even though it's January, but something at the very center of my body misses the slushy brown streets in Chicago which makes no sense but reminds me of what Mr. McInnis said a long time ago about leaving a place before you can be proud of it. He feels very far away. I lay my head on Mom's shoulder. "Tired?" she asks and I say yes (which you're supposed to say instead of *yeah* in Alabama) because it's the easiest thing.

• • •

I wake up under a quilt with frayed edges and colorful stars on Fuzzy's couch, which is old but not scratchy and doesn't smell like medicine like I thought. I fell asleep after Fuzzy made a breakfast bigger than I've ever had, with eggs and bacon and grits, which didn't taste like much by themselves but Fuzzy told me to mix everything together 'cause that's how God intended breakfast, so I did, and then they tasted good and I started to feel better about things but also exhausted.

The sun is slanting through the front window in strong stripes. I should get up but my arms and legs are rocks and my mouth is dry from sleeping at the wrong time like a mixed-up owl. I can see Fuzzy on the front porch whistling and sweeping and I listen for a while. Every few sweeps Fuzzy spits into the front yard. Tommy coughs and Mom murmurs from somewhere in the back of the little house. A black and white clock in the shape of a cat is ticking on the wall and I wonder if it's the same time in Chicago and if it is, what Marisol is doing at 1:21 p.m. in Ms. Sanogo's class. Probably math. "She doesn't even know I'm gone," I say to no one. But it's Marisol, so she might.

"Hey, bright eyes," Fuzzy says when I walk onto the porch and sit on the swing, still wrapped in stars. "Your mama still sleepin'?"

I shrug. "I think so."

Fuzzy whistles with his teeth, the way he did on the phone when I told him I was eleven. "Must have been quite a trip." He checks his watch. "How 'bout you and me run down to the curb market quick and pick up some eggs?"

I blink at him because I don't understand what

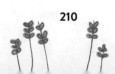

a curb market is or how anyone at this house could possibly eat more eggs. Then I say, "Okay."

Fuzzy writes a note to Mom and I smile at his handwriting because really it's what brought us here in the first place. We climb back into the truck and this time I roll my window down too and hang my hand out waving and everyone waves back. "Uncle Fuzzy?" I ask.

"Yes, ma'am."

"What are you gonna do with more eggs?"

Fuzzy smiles at me with his changing skies eyes. "I'm gonna bake y'all a cake."

I've never heard of a man baking a cake but it seems like something Tonio would do. "Why?" I ask.

"'Cause that's what you do when family comes. Like to do a pound cake if I can get some duck eggs. Fella always holds some for me but the market's fixin' to close so we'll see." I have so many questions I don't know where to start so I just ride along, bumping over potholes, which for some reason makes me want to laugh out loud.

• • •

The curb market turns out to be a building with no walls which answers my question *Is there winter in Alabama?* because if there was the snow would blow right in and cover everyone's vegetables and soup jars and cakes with a million layers. There's a cold breeze but no one's wearing winter hats so I guess they don't know any better or maybe they don't have any. And they're not shaking out their hands or stomping their feet like we do in Chicago. They're sitting still as rocks like waiting for it to end.

I follow Fuzzy down the main aisle looking back and forth trying to see everything because I'm used to collecting information even though I guess I don't need to now. There's lots of things I've never seen, like jars filled with yellow stuff called chow chow and plates of divinity, which might be made out of marshmallows. But mostly it's familiar stuff like carrots and onions and broccoli. I think of Faiza saying *Fruits and vegetables and mostly vegetables!*

She would like this place. That's another person I'll never see again.

"Mostly greens this time of year," Fuzzy says. "Just wait till the peaches come in. Can't hardly walk through here. 'Less you got a stick."

He says *Hey!* to everyone and *War Eagle!* to some people and they all smile at me but I feel them wondering who I am and I'm wondering too. We make it to the end of the aisle where a lady sits wrapped in a blanket covered with old-fashioned tigers and that's another thing I'll have to learn because all I know is Bears and Bulls and Blackhawks.

"Hey, Fuzzy," she says.

"Hey, doll. Where's Roland at?"

"Stayed home today. Too cold for his skinny britches. I told him he needs more meat on his bones like me. I stay nice and toasty." She laughs. "Who's this pretty thing?"

"This here's Jane's granddaughter, Brittany."

Her eyes brighten like those light switches you can click up. Marisol has one in her living room but

it's usually on the lowest spot. For no reason I think of her dad Ending It All and wonder if they found him on the living room couch. In the bright light or the medium or the dim.

"Is that the truth!" the lady says. "I'm Moxie! Jane and I were girls together!" She comes out of her booth and gives me a big hug. "I'm so glad to see you, shug! You here with your mama?"

"Yes, ma'am."

"Well, we are so happy to have y'all."

I don't know what to say so I say, "Thanks."

Fuzzy pays for his duck eggs (which are enormous) while I stare at rows of hair bows laid out on a white cloth that remind me of Marisol's hair ribbons and my sea glass and all the art I had to leave behind, still taped to my walls unless Jack ripped it down. Mom said Laila would get it for us but I know she won't.

"My daughter makes those," Moxie says. "Go ahead and pick you one." I look at Fuzzy and he nods and starts to pull out his wallet but Moxie waves it away. I choose the only yellow one, like my Plan B notebook, like *wheat fields waving,* but much softer, more like the very early morning sun in Chicago.

The market's closing down all around us when we walk back through, all the vegetables going back in their crates and the cakes back in their boxes. "Bet your mom's awake by now," Fuzzy says. "Time to show y'all your new house!" We climb into the truck and I bounce on the springs like a little kid because it's starting to feel like my spot. The yellow bow is still in my fist and I should have said to Moxie, *I'm happy to have y'all too.*

Seventeen

Mom's standing in front of the tall mirror, which is still cloudy even though I sprayed it with so much Windex it dripped on the floor before I could wipe it all. She's tucking and untucking the shirt she just ironed, which is made out of church fabric and has a curved collar like a flower petal.

"What do you think?" she asks.

"Tucked."

She tucks it back in and slips on the high heels from the thrift store and when she walks to the dresser her skirt sways, just like Odessa said dresses did in the olden days when she rocked her knuckly hand on the front porch with the plants spinning in the wind. I miss her but not as much as I miss Marisol. She's called me twice, and hearing her voice on Tonio's phone is both happy and sad, like walking by a classroom you grew out of where the kindergartners are still cutting with round scissors and their tongues are sticking out.

I'm lying on my stomach on Granny's bed, which now belongs to Mom, watching emojis from Laila pop up one by one on Mom's phone: smiley faces and hearts and kisses and flowers and a thumbs-up and a tube of lipstick. And finally a trophy, like Mom already got the job. Granny's bedspread is covered in huge white flowers that remind me of Georgia O'Keeffe. Mom breathes out and says, "Okay. I'm ready."

I look up and she's beautiful. She's wearing clip-on earrings she found in Granny's drawer that are like little red fireworks. They're so old-fashioned they'd be ridiculous on anyone else but on Mom they're perfect, like Agata's glasses. But it's not just the earrings or her hair blow-dried straight and curled at the bottom or her new lipstick. It's something else. Something about how her heels sound clicking on the wood floors.

"You look amazing," I tell her. "Your posture is just like Granny's."

"Aww. Thanks, sweet pea." She kisses me on the forehead. "When Tommy wakes up give him a snack, okay? There's applesauce in the fridge."

"Okay."

She picks up her phone and walks out of the room but then leans back in. "Why don't you write Mr. McInnis a letter?" she asks.

"Huh?"

"I'm sure he'd like to hear from you."

"Mom. You're so old-school. No one writes letters anymore."

"Well, they should. Getting mail is nice."

I think of Fuzzy's big pink envelope in the middle of all that junk, saving our lives. "Maybe I will."

• • •

Dear Mr. McInnis,

This is Brittany Kowalski. I wanted to write just to let you know I'm safe. Not that you would be worried but just in case. We're in Montgomery, Alabama. We rode a bus here and it took seventeen hours.

We're living in my granny's old house. It's a little white house with a saggy front porch and when we walked inside my mom sighed super deep and said <u>Jesus,</u> because it really was a mess. But we started cleaning it up and it's not so bad. My uncle Fuzzy comes over every day to help or bring collards from his garden. He's old but strong. Have you ever had collards? Mom says they're an "<u>acquired taste</u>" but Tommy already loves them! (That's my little brother. He can walk now. He took his first step on the front porch, which is amazing because like I said it's very saggy.)

Also the church ladies help a lot. We went to Granny's church last Sunday and since then I swear a church lady comes over with food every day. Our refrigerator got so full Mom brought half of it to Miss Sula across the street. She has an old gray cat with one eye named Sweetie who scares the mailman so bad he delivers the mail to Granny's house and Miss Sula comes over to pick it up, or sometimes I bring it to her because Sweetie likes me.

My new school's fine but everyone knows I'm different because I don't have an accent. It's hard to fit in when every time you open your mouth you sound like a plain mouse. Plus I miss your art lessons (except for Kandinsky, no offense). My new teacher just teaches regular things. Mom says to give it time and that there's nothing more important than being at peace in the world. As Uncle Fuzzy would say, "Ain't that the plain truth."

Sincerely,
Brittany Kowalski

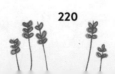

P.S. The painting is of our new house in four different kinds of light (like Monet).

P.P.S. Please don't give up on the aquarium. I know you'll get there someday.

acknowledgments

I'm thankful for so many. This list is just the start.

Thanks to my incredibly kind and insightful editor, Wendy Loggia, for pausing one morning in the mailroom, and then bringing a vague idea to life. I will never love anyone's emails more than yours. To Delacorte Press. To Maria Middleton for the lovely design and Jori van der Linde for the beautiful art. To Jessica Maria Tuccelli for teaching me the publishing ropes and Cara Thaxton for helping me remember Chicago.

Thanks to the teachers who encouraged me and made me better: Barb Lykken, Marilyn Teubert, Kari Stringer, Patricia Strandness, Don Rogan, P. F. Kluge, Conner Bailey. To Barbara Bellucci and all of my victim advocate colleagues for your mentorship and for teaching me what I needed to know.

To my amazing friends: Corby Baumann for being my Marisol. Thkisha Sanogo, who believed in me when I needed it the absolute most. Ashley Cauley, for making this ride insanely fun to share. Jennifer Yeager, Carin Brock, Ali Bolton, Melissa Shaver, Valerie Downes, and Heather Smith, who helped me celebrate every step.

To Regina Benjamin, Julie Taylor, and Beverly Dean, who had faith in me before I had faith in myself. You mean more to me than you can know.

And to my family: Aunt Bonnie, for loving books and loving me. Mom, for every single thing. Dad, Mag, and Sam, for teaching me what family means and cheering me on no matter what. Stan, Andrew, Leo, and Katie, who fill up my whole heart every single day. I could not be more proud of you or more honored to be your mom. And to Andre. Everything is possible because you told me so, and everything is sweet because of you.

about the author

Emily Blejwas grew up in Minnesota and now lives in Mobile, Alabama, with her husband and four children. She directs the Gulf States Health Policy Center, has worked in the fields of community development and victim advocacy, and holds degrees from Auburn University and Kenyon College. This is her first novel.

emilyblejwas.com
facebook.com/emilyblejwas ▊
emilyblejwas ▣
@EmilyBlejwas ▾